Dallas

"I see we have a new student with us today — Tex Dobson."

"Yes, sir," the new boy in the front row said, his voice low, almost shy. He was tall, so tall that his lean legs in faded jeans and old cowboy boots stuck out into the aisle. The girl several seats behind him was unable to see his face, but the back of his neck was a ruddy brown, crisscrossed with the weather marks of hot suns and strong winds. Big-shouldered, hunched over the small desk, he might have been an older man, someone just visiting the classroom, but his words were young, respectful, and carefully courteous.

"I've been called Tex, sir," he said. "And I guess my father might have registered me that way, but now that I'm here, and back in school, I'd like to go by my given name."

"All right. What's that?" Mr. Engel asked.

"I was christened 'Dallas,'" the boy said

**Other Point paperbacks
you will want to read:**

point

ACTS OF LOVE

Maureen Daly

SCHOLASTIC INC.
New York Toronto London Auckland Sydney

ISBN 0-590-43631-7

12 11 10 9 8 7 6 5 4 3 2 1   0 1 2 3 4 5/9

Printed in the U.S.A.   01

With thoughts of Megan, always. And with special thanks to Jan and Ken Stelter of the Arriba Arabian Stud and Equestrian Center of Thousand Palms, California, for their information and for coming to Dallas Dobson's help when he needed them most.

ACTS OF LOVE

. . . that best portion of a good man's life,
His little, nameless, unremembered, acts
Of kindness and of love.

William Wordsworth

Chapter
1

Most important things don't happen overnight, at least the things that change lives. Henrietta Caldwell didn't know that. And her mother, if she did know, chose not to say anything, at least not until near the end.

With the new highway, there had been flags of warning, the first surveyors' stakes stuck into the ground, slim wooden shafts tied at one end with a little flutter of red cloth. Those telltale stakes traced a pathway through the woods and meadows, almost cutting the Caldwell lands in half. They started at the property line down behind the pond and ended at the top of the meadow near the big dead oak, a

3

split, gray tree that had been struck by winter lightning some years ago.

It took the young girl more than three hours, that early spring day she had first sighted the red flags. Snow was still on the ground, but there was the sound of water just beginning to run under the thick brook ice.

Anger gave her energy. With wet, cold hands, Retta pulled out every stake, dumping armload after armload on the front terrace. How had someone dared to walk over those fields and lay claim to land that belonged only to the Caldwells?

Ever since the days when William Penn was the first governor of Pennsylvania, a Caldwell had built and lived on that property — a span of almost three hundred years. The present Caldwell family still owned more than forty acres, and Henrietta and her young brother were familiar with every rocky mica pit and ivy-covered fence on the property. No one had to tell them at what side of the brook the first green-leafed arum broke through crusty ground in spring. Nor that the stretch of glade between the old apple trees was the best spot for a salt lick for young deer. And they had decided for themselves that the hillock beside the big oak, sprinkled with corn feed, would attract flocks of autumn geese that honked down from Canada with the first frost.

Everyone in Zenith and around the countryside knew the Carter Caldwells (when Carter Caldwell himself was a boy, and for generations before, the family was known as "those really rich Caldwells"), and present-day Zenith residents could still point out which fields and woodlands remained as part of "the old Caldwell place."

She had been young that fateful spring, just a few weeks past fourteen, and her father had tried to explain to her just why the red flags were there.

The whole program was still in the discussion stages, he said, but the State Highway Commission had selected twenty acres of Caldwell land as part of a new multimillion-dollar bypass system, a proposed six-lane highway to loop around Zenith and make way for the freight trucks and heavy-vehicle traffic going to Baltimore or Philadelphia. There would be town meetings pro and con, her father told her, and the family was getting legal advice from local lawyers, but under the statute of "Right of Eminent Domain," the state of Pennsylvania had the authority to do what it had done — in planting the stakes — at least for now.

"Laws are made by men, and laws must be obeyed by men," her father had said at the dinner table. "But this family isn't through fighting, not by a long shot."

Within days, the highway crew was back at work and new little red flags were set in place, like brilliant, hated flowers, staking claim through meadow, woods, and orchard.

But the other thing, the thing involving the new person, was different. There had been no warning at all.

It was early fall, more than two years later. Henrietta was sixteen and in her third year of high school.

Even though he was technically a senior, the young man had missed a lot of school and was assigned to work for needed catch-up credits with a junior geometry class.

The weather was hot and hazy, full of smells of the countryside still touched with summer and vacation freedom, the way September can be in rural Pennsylvania.

Through the half-opened windows of the classroom, the odor of gasoline and warm rubber drifted in from the crowded parking lot. There were four big yellow school buses for crossroads pickups, but anyone at Havendale High with a driver's license preferred his own car. Junior Provanza's new Porsche sat under a small sycamore tree, the turning leaves casting dappled shadows over the bright red paint and the smooth, black upholstery. This was a consolidated county high school and some of the students lived on working farms, but most had parents with homes and a job in the small, nearby town of Zenith, with some commuting to employment in Wilmington or even downtown Philadelphia, thirty-five miles away.

Junior Provanza worked weekends and after school at his father's general store at Millstream Crossroads, and on Saturdays he cut meat for the butcher section. Some of the wealthier students had a different life-style and even rode their own horses to school in good weather, stabling the animals during the day at old Mrs. Curtayne's barns just down the road. The student body was a mixed group. Junior

Provanza strongly felt the status need of his bright new car.

Before the final attendance bell, someone had smeared the inside panes of a rear window with a cut-up apple or pear and now, during class, a half dozen black-and-yellow wasps bobbed and bumped against the glass. The insects were the dominant females, drowsy now, bodies heavy and pendulous, already ready to hive-up for the winter. Yet there was something sensual and demanding in the rhythmic drone, the way the wasps were so persistently drawn to the promise of fruity smells and sweet juices. No one can be sure, however, whether or not an autumn wasp may have one last sting.

But Mr. Engel, the math teacher, was not ready to clear the classroom because of the old wasp trick. He himself had been a student at Havendale High when it was only six classrooms and a cow pasture for a baseball field. And he believed the insects, torpid and slow-flying, were not likely to leave the sticky sweetness of the window panes for an attack. So he settled behind his desk, studied the roll book, and said firmly, "I see we have a new student with us today — Tex Dobson."

"Yes, sir," the new boy in the front row said, his voice low, almost shy. He was tall, so tall that his lean legs in faded jeans and old cowboy boots stuck out into the aisle. The girl several seats behind him was unable to see his face, but the back of his neck was a ruddy brown, crisscrossed with the weather marks of hot suns and strong winds. Big-shouldered, hunched over the small desk, he might have been an older man, someone just visiting the classroom, but his words were young, respectful, and carefully courteous.

"I've been called Tex, sir," he said. "And I guess my father might have registered me that way, but now that I'm here, and back in school, I'd like to go by my given name."

"All right. What's that?" Mr. Engel asked.

"I was christened 'Dallas,' " the boy said.

There was a swift, taut silence in the classroom, a void of movement or sound that meant that everyone was about to laugh, if only someone else dared to laugh first.

Mr. Engel was quick to comprehend and said matter-of-factly, "Thank you, Dallas Dobson. And since you're so tall, I'd appreciate it if you would take a desk in the back of the classroom. There's one right behind Henrietta Caldwell, the girl in the blue blouse. I'll speak to you right after class, Dallas, to find out where and on what you need to catch up. I don't think we have a problem."

In a seat across the aisle, Charlotte Amberson twisted around to stare full-face at Henrietta. There was a small, enigmatic smile on her lips, but Henrietta could not read her friend's eyes. Ever since early summer, and now right up into the first of the school year, Charlie Amberson had affected huge sunglasses, both by day and by night. She had managed to buy herself an extensive collection, and today the dark circles of glass were framed in blue denim, matching her jeans and jacket. Even though the glasses revealed nothing, her soft, curved mouth seemed to be saying, "Well, all right!"

As the person called Dallas Dobson gathered together his books, Retta Caldwell turned her glance away from his big shoulders and the shaggy hairline ragged over the sun-browned neck, and forced herself to look down at the floor. As the young man passed her desk, she noticed the boots again, calf-high with narrow, stacked heels. On the maroon leather uppers there was a little flag of Texas, embossed with metallic color, on the outer ankle. Although they had the dulled sheen of a recent rub down with saddle soap, the leather was creased and worn and, as Dobson walked quickly to the back of the room, his boots made a slipping, squeaking sound on the polished floor.

For a moment, Retta felt a stab of near dislike toward her best friend, Charlie Amberson, with the opaque eyes and evaluating, sensual smile on her lips. *Charlie, give the guy a chance,* she thought.

The desk chair behind her creaked with Dobson's rangy body weight, and Retta was aware that the new boy must now be staring at her — her straight back, the short red curl of her hair, the narrow collar of her new blouse.

She stifled a sigh, so quickly and completely that it almost brought tears to her eyes. *He's probably got cotton stuffed in those toes,* the girl in the blue blouse thought with a mixture of sadness and warmth. *Or maybe just a bunch of scrunched-up straw from somebody's barn.* His first day in a new school, his first chance to make an impression on the class, and this new person was trying to make it in old, borrowed clothes. No polite "sirs" to Mr. Engel, no extra buffing of the shoes, not even the tarnished Texas stars could change that. This guy was hurting.

Retta Caldwell knew those boots were not really his, that they had once belonged to someone else.

Ordinarily, dinnertime was the best hour of the day at the Caldwells', a time to talk, discuss, or just laugh. They usually dined at seven o'clock, just as the chimes struck on the hall clock, and even though the food might be heated leftovers, the serving dishes sat on old silver trivets. There was a decorative crystal bowl in the center of the table, filled, according to season, with wildflowers or pine cones. Most nights a pair of candles lit the table. Tonight the candles were unlit and a warm fall breeze blew through the opened windows, a wind scented with dry leaves and the faint, ammonia odor of steer manure the yardman had dug in around the asparagus beds. Yet Retta felt a rare and worrisome tension in the beamed dining room, a silence that was deliberate rather than accidental, and she looked sharply at her father and then her mother.

Connie Caldwell was as slim as her daughter, but with dark hair tied back in a ponytail with a string of green yarn. She wore jeans and a green sweater with a pink shirt showing at the neck and cuffs.

"You're very preppy tonight, Mother," Retta said. "You look ready to enroll at Radcliffe."

"Your mother was pretty *and preppy* before that

10

word was born," Carter Caldwell said.

Her mother's answer was unexpectedly short and sharp. "Sweet of you, dear," she said. "But not true. Sometimes looking preppy just means forgetting to put on lipstick, or having to always wear the same old clothes."

"What I meant . . ." Henrietta began, but her mother smiled and passed a plate of beef and mushroom casserole. "Hand this on down to your father. And don't worry about my mood. This hasn't been the best possible day."

The phone in the hallway rang, two short rings to show it was for the Caldwell household, the first party on a three-party line. Henrietta, putting down her fork and turning to her brother, said, "Will you answer that, Two? It has to be Charlie. No one else would be stupid enough to call me during dinnertime."

As her younger brother hurried toward the hallway, Retta said to her father, "That certainly can't count as one of my two calls for tonight. You know how crazy and irresponsible Charlotte can be. . . ."

"It won't count," her father said laconically.

When Henrietta turned sixteen and her brother was nearly eleven, the Caldwell house had become a sudden maelstrom, with the telephone ringing a dozen times a day. So one evening, a few months earlier, the family had a one-sided conference. Carter Caldwell, Senior (Carter Caldwell, Junior, was always called Two) made an announcement at dinner: "From now on, each of you children can receive two incoming calls a day, and you can make four

11

outgoing calls if you like, except, of course, long distance. On charge calls, check with your mother and me. We're not going to have our lives disrupted with all the nonsensical calls you get," he said with finality.

She had laughed aloud, Retta remembered. Her father's face had been so stern, so determined, just like those old pictures in the upstairs hallway when he was a solemn little boy taking horseback riding lessons.

"No need for you to get so fierce about it," she had told him. "Two and I won't have any trouble. We'll just tell everyone our father is a first-class eccentric."

Caldwell had smiled. "We're going to be a much happier family all around if you have more trouble handling *me* than your mother and I have handling you."

Her brother came back to the table. "You were right, Retta. That *was* Charlie. She says you know what she wants to talk about. . . ."

Retta went to the kitchen for the dessert tray: four plates of plain sliced cake ready for a spoonful of wineberries and a pitcher of cream. It was not a family favorite; not that the dessert didn't taste good, but it was economy food and they had it often. Wineberries grew wild along the country lanes in the summertime, brambled bushes weighted down with wine-red fruit. Country folk around Zenith didn't respect the berry much because it was runny when cooked and wouldn't set at all for jellies and jams. But the Caldwell children picked basketfuls every

12

July and August to stock the freezer.

Once, a few years ago, the family-owned newspaper was making higher profits. The Caldwells still had daily household help, and young Two — not even old enough to go to school — had said to Aunt Blue, a respected old black lady who came in to do the cleaning and cooking, that he didn't like wineberries, they were nothing but second-class raspberries, or blackberries without guts. Aunt Blue had gone into a rage and ordered Two to leave her kitchen "which is as much God's temple as any church on earth." But when she heard him crying out on the back doorstep, she went out to hug him and rock him on her knee, saying, "I just get frightened sometimes when I hear young people too proud to thank the Good Lord for what He puts on earth every summer."

Her mother's mother had died long before Retta was born, yet it always seemed to her she still had two grandmothers. Grandmama Caldwell was a very real person, a tiny, fine-voiced woman with blue-gray hair, who came to her son's family on twice-yearly visits and whose letters from Florida, thin and spidery scrawls on pale beige notepaper, never failed to enclose two crisp five-dollar bills, one for Retta and one for her brother. Once Henrietta had asked her father why Grandmama Caldwell's money felt so silky, seemed so different, and he had told her with a laugh, "You'll find this hard to believe, but your grandmother washes out those five-dollar bills in her bathroom hand basin and irons them flat before mailing them. And she even sprinkles on a little of her lilac cologne. She told me herself. Even if she can't see them as often as she'd like, she wants everything to be perfect for her grandchildren, the sweet old dear."

It was Aunt Blue who seemed to be the other grandmother. It was she who let the young Caldwells press raisin faces into the cookie dough before she baked it; carved the scariest faces on November pumpkins; and walked Retta and Two through the old herb garden again and again till they both could tell the difference between basil and tarragon, parsley and cilantro, and lemon mint from the finger sprigs of garden mint that went into iced tea. She had taught them to be kind to all three cats and give each one an equal hug at bedtime. She showed them how to count to ten and then start laughing, instead of getting hurt feelings and running sulking to their rooms. She often turned the Bible station on the kitchen radio down to a background murmur and told the children little singsong stories about herself, her own childhood, and her life down in the deep South. "Start out wise," she told them repeatedly. "Learn to take a little bad with the good. I did that, and pretty soon I got good most of the time."

Retta had been aware, even as a young girl, that she loved both old ladies, though for different reasons, but when she thought of grandmothers, it was almost always Aunt Blue who came to life first in her thoughts.

Now the wineberries seemed a symbol. *A little bad with the good,* Retta thought as she spooned the soft, half-frozen berries onto the cake, the juice

thin and staining. It seemed to her the Carter Caldwells were having wineberries more and more lately.
Almost every night, in fact.

As she backed her way through the swinging doors
to the dining room, holding the tray, she heard her
father say, "Well, Connie, if Hugo Provanza wants
to drop his weekly ad, I appreciate that he came in
to tell me about it in person."

His wife's voice was distressed. "But the Provanzas have run that full-page ad in the *Zenith Press*
every week since I was a little girl. Did he say why
he — "

"Our paper just isn't reaching the right people
anymore, Connie. Hugo says he gets a better response on his ad if he just makes it a throwaway to
stick in mailboxes. Not everyone subscribes to the
Press these days, you know."

Caldwell shook his head at his daughter. "Pass
me by, Retta. Maybe Two wants an extra dessert.
Or I'll have mine later with the eleven o'clock news."

"That's partly the trouble, isn't it?" Two said. "Small-
town papers don't matter much anymore, do they?
All the big stuff is on TV, anyway."

"Not quite *all* the big stuff, Two. And the shopping
malls in Wilmington and Philadelphia are boom-
ing." He was answering his son, but seemed to be
addressing himself more directly to his wife. "Hugo
Provanza told me a bit of news today that I could
never get from any TV commentator. He's decided
he needs a lawyer from Philadelphia to help him
out on this highway thing, someone really smart.
We're not the only ones who could be hurt. If that

15

bypass goes through, it could cut the Provanza property in two, with their house on one side of the road and the store on the other. He said it would be better for him if the six-lane highway could go through his buildings, not between them. Then they'd have to pay him for the loss of the house *and* his business, not just some pittance for the land they take. Either way, it's a bad deal for him."

The rest of the evening was serene, almost as peaceful and silent as the dark woods beyond the living room windows. Two made a couple of phone calls and got two back, but they lasted only a few seconds each with conversations that seemed to be no more than, "Hi ya," then a couple of chuckles, and an, "Okay, see you tomorrow."

Retta curled in a corner chair, leafing through a Spanish edition of *Jane Eyre*. It was her favorite book, and the familiar English words seemed to shine out through the Spanish, almost whispering the magic story as she turned the pages. She had decided not to call Charlie back.

Her parents sat in wicker-basket chairs at a round table, playing chess. When the late news came on TV, they stopped playing, their hands still on the chessboard, fingers touching lightly.

Later that night, so late that she wasn't sure what time it was, Retta heard the phone ring in the upstairs hallway outside her bedroom, then the scurry of feet as Two leaped out of bed to answer it.

There was a mumble of voices and Two called out, "Don't worry, Dad. A man asked who it was and when I told him my name, he hung up. Must have been a wrong number."

Her father's voice was low but clear as he called out from behind his closed bedroom door. "All right, Two. Let's say it *was* a wrong number. But if the phone rings again — this time of night — let me answer it."

Retta's senses sharpened as she heard the warning tone in her father's voice. She noticed a fine line of light limned along the narrow windowsill of her bedroom, just under the hem of the red draperies. It could be moonlight, or it could be the first early rays of dawn coming over the horizon. Before Retta could decide, she was asleep again, and as far as she knew, the phone did not ring again.

Chapter
2

All over the United States, towns like Cleveland, Amarillo, and Gary, Indiana, kept getting bigger and bigger with more people and more houses, even though Zenith, Pennsylvania, which was older than any of them, kept getting smaller and smaller. Once, about a hundred and fifty years ago, the same era the Caldwell family founded their newspaper, the *Zenith Press,* the town had its own hotel. Zenith was a railroad passenger stop for travelers en route from Washington and Baltimore to Philadelphia. The Zenith Arms had been a small, perfect hotel with a wide veranda with rocking chairs and gentlemen from the South in white gloves to serve tea or mint juleps while the ladies of the party freshened up.

Without a dining car on the train, passengers always dined on chicken and biscuits at the Zenith Arms before huffing and chugging the last thirty-five miles into Philadelphia.

About ten thousand people lived in and around Zenith then, the in-town merchants in their big clapboard houses along the main streets; the Quakers out on prosperous farms, the fields as precise and neat as homemade quilts. The "gentlemen farms" were for the really rich, with long, green barns, split-rail fences, and hunting mares brought in from Kentucky and Ireland.

Some of old Zenith was still there. The railroad depot had been torn down years ago, and the old hotel was now a retirement home for Sisters of the Order of Mercy. But there was still a post office and a volunteer fire department, the only two buildings that always flew an American flag, regardless of regulations, in both sunshine and rain. Many of the grand old merchants' houses had been divided into apartments, and the only movie house had closed down just as soon as a drive-in opened in Wilmington. But the main street was three blocks long with a drugstore, an appliance emporium, four men's apparel shops, and a few stores to sell almost anything one might need, if you didn't mind limited stock.

About a half dozen shops already had gone out of business, plate-glass windows facing the street boarded over. The gray stone building that housed the *Zenith Press* was as graceful and staunch as ever, but there were failed businesses on either side of it. The main street of Zenith had become a major thoroughfare, bumper-to-bumper on Saturday mostly with shoppers headed for the malls of Wilmington, or even Philadelphia.

"I get so angry sometimes, I could just cry," Retta had said to her mother only last year. "I looked up Zenith in the atlas and it's a little nothing, just a name so small an ant couldn't read it. It's like marrying a dwarf or having a darling baby brother with two heads. Don't those stupid atlas people know we love this town? It's not a fly-speck dot on the map to us."

"Just don't bring the subject up at the dinner table," her mother had said. "Nor the fact that Ye Olde Butterchurn is moving into the Wilmington Mall. Your father knows all about those things. Ads at the newspaper are down about fifty-five percent this year. Even all the local sports coverage, my editorials, and that crazy social stuff Charlotte's mother writes — well, it gets us some new readers and a few phone calls, but the advertising revenues just aren't there like the old days."

"But Poppy always wanted us to be open about what we thought," Retta protested. "Why can't I tell him how I feel about Zenith?"

"Just give him a chance to rearrange his priorities," her mother said. "Caldwells aren't good at being failures. Your father is awfully hard on himself these days. . . ."

Charlotte Amberson (nicknamed "Charlie" because her mother's name was also Charlotte) had been Retta Caldwell's best friend since fourth grade. Charlie liked to tease and often said Retta had an A-average in school only because she got up so early each morning. And Mrs. Amberson remarked sharply one day that "God just gave the lucky little blue-blood a twenty-six-hour day, while the rest of us peasants do our best on twenty-four."

The simple truth was that Henrietta Caldwell loved to get up at dawn. Even on the darkest winter morning, when the weather was so full of wind and blown snow that the upstairs windows coated over, she enjoyed the challenge of a cold floor and a quiet house. It was always Retta who tiptoed down first to plug in the coffee maker, feed the dogs, and turn up the thermostat. Mornings worked for her and she worked well in the mornings. And she liked the extra time to be Henrietta Caldwell, herself and alone.

In past years, after Aunt Blue had retired and lived in a small house about two miles down Tuckpoint Road, and when the weather was right, Retta used the early hours to bicycle over the graveled roads to check on the old lady. She had a key to let herself in.

Aunt Blue, three times married but with no children, insisted on living alone without a dog, a TV set, or even a telephone. "If anything that ain't in my Bible happens out there in the big world," she said once, "I can trust Henrietta to ride over and tell me."

On that last day, Retta would always remember, the old house seemed unusually still. A clock ticked somewhere and Aunt Blue's harmonica was sitting

21

on the newel post of the staircase, an odd place for it to be. But the silence was a special silence.

Aunt Blue had died sometime in the night and Retta found her in bed, hands folded on the chenille bedspread which was turned down as neatly and precisely as if it had been measured with a ruler.

Aunt Blue had been brought up in a convent in Gethsemane, Kentucky, and she loved to tell about those days, while sipping tea in the Caldwell kitchen and massaging her firm, red gums with a snuff stick.

"Our rooms were set up in the old slave cottages behind the main convent," she had told them, "all fancied up with curtains and rag rugs. In early times, young white ladies who wanted to become nuns could bring slave girls as their dowry for entering the order. They didn't need to bring money or family jewels — just a couple of black girls the family owned.

"Retta, when you study in school, you'll find that history don't go back as far as you think. My own great-grandmother was a slave, one of those girls brought in as dowry, and that's how I got to live the orphanage life. When I got bigger, they hired me out to do day work, but I was born and reared behind that convent.

"It's God's way that babies just keep coming, so by the time black folk weren't slaves anymore, there were so many orphans that the girls had to sleep four to a bed. I was always a neat sleeper. That's how the nuns taught me. I was so well trained that in my whole life I never turned over in bed once."

Retta remembered vividly that Aunt Blue had

seemed perplexed and silent for a moment, and then she added, "I'm not talking about *marrying*-turning over, Retta. I'm talking about *sleeping*-turning over." Then she said severely, "You don't have to ask me no questions. You be a good girl and your mother will tell you everything you need to know when the time comes. . . ."

Her real name was Mrs. Paula Saint-Scales, and Retta knew that was the name her mother would use when she wrote the obituary. Only the Caldwells had called the old lady Aunt Blue. It was a nickname born because Mrs. Saint-Scales had a deep and almost religious conviction that there wasn't enough blue in the world.

"The Good Lord must have been partial to blue," she had explained, "or He wouldn't have used it so much for the sky. When it came to food, He got distracted." So Mrs. Saint-Scales preserved at least a quart of dark blue elderberry juice each summer, and used it to color certain foods throughout the year.

"It's a derbyberry anyway," she had explained to Two, with some heat. "How can folks call it an 'elderberry' if they don't have no 'youngerberry'? Makes no sense. At least where I come from, folks know what to *call* things."

It was never potatoes or fish or cauliflower that turned up blue at the Caldwell dinner table, but it might be a pie crust, a pear compote, or a tray of hot blue muffins on the sideboard on a Sunday.

Now Henrietta touched the old lady's folded hands and found them soft but chill. There was peace here, no anger, no protest, no struggling against the end. Pride had stayed with the old woman until the last.

Henrietta felt an instinctive thing she must do. Aunt Blue would want to be free now, really free — girlhood, pig-tailed, Kentucky-blue grass-free.

She opened all the windows in the bedroom so the spring breezes could blow in and out across the bed, ruffling what they wanted, bringing odors of dew and saplings and green things growing. Dawn was just beginning to touch color to the horizon, a glowing pink, pale still but clear. It would be a day of cloudless skies.

It was weeks later, long after the burial in Holly Hill Cemetery, that Retta discovered Aunt Blue's house key. In the strange excitement of that morning, she had zipped the key into the inner compartment of her school purse. And, for reasons she did not quite know, she decided to keep it there.

The compact yellow Volkswagen, with 62,000 miles on the odometer but a new set of tires, had been a semi-surprise on Retta's sixteenth birthday. She had already taken drivers' education at school and for years she'd been allowed to drive the family car over the meadow to the pond for winter skating. Connie Caldwell had lived in Zenith as a girl, not far from a skating rink, and the younger Caldwells had been taught to skate when they were just children. It was usually Retta who drove the station wagon down to the pond on an icy morning with fried-egg sandwiches and a thermos of coffee.

She had passed her driver's test in Coatesville on her first try.

Charlie Amberson had given her a Swift 'N Sweet floral kit for the car as a birthday present, a can of lilac-jasmine spray that made the interior smell like a deodorized women's rest room at Penn Station. Retta stored the can in the glove compartment.

Two had bought her a tiny, female religious figure, garbed in blue, and hung it in the back window of the Volkswagen, insisting it was a replica of the patron saint of bullfighters, the Virgin of Macerena.

"Who knows, *bonita*," he said. "The beautiful Señorita Caldwell might just be lucky enough to pick up some hitchhiking *torero*."

"You've got the wrong *señorita*," Retta said with a laugh. "I don't know how Poppy feels about bullfighters, but I *do* know how he feels about hitchhikers. He gave me a big no on that even before he turned over the keys."

It was six months after she got the yellow car and her license, and just the day after she'd seen Dallas Dobson for the first time, that she saw him for the second time. Or thought she did.

With her driver's license had come her first job. Five mornings a week, before school, she drove over to the Armstrong house to pick up the society column, "Chatter by Char," that Charlie's mother wrote for the Caldwell paper. The column, full of local chitchat, horse meets, church suppers, engagements, and weddings, was currently the most popular feature in the paper. Carter Caldwell had hired Charlotte Amberson right after she had left her third husband for the last time. Mrs. Amberson needed the work and turned out to be good at it, gathering most of the news by phone, then delivering the copy herself.

But in the last few months, she had not felt able to drive into Zenith. It wasn't because of the late hours she kept, or even the frequent sips of fine Madeira she poured from the decanter, Mrs. Amberson insisted.

"The belle of the county has lost some zip," she had told Carter Caldwell. "I've developed a phobia. Not *agoraphobia*, mind you, nothing radical like that. I have a *controlled* phobia. It's all enemy territory out there until after three in the afternoon."

So Retta did the daily pickup and delivery every morning between seven and the first eight o'clock class at Havendale High.

This morning, too early for Mrs. Amberson, she was meandering along the country roads to pass time. Retta drove slowly, almost daydreaming, listening to the rhythmic sing of the tires on the gravel, yet keeping her eyes alert to the mists ahead. Typical of Pennsylvania in autumn, an early mist rose from the roadside grass and bushes, a miasmic fog that moved upward and began to evaporate into the growing warmth of the morning, almost as if it left the ground.

She was on a narrow back lane with barely room for two cars to pass. On either side of the road were ditches still thick with the grass of summer and

26

patches of broad-leafed sumac, the dusty leaves barely touched with the rusts of fall.

These roads were familiar to Retta and she didn't need a map to know where she had been or what lay ahead. She knew she was not far from the old Kennelly farm, neglected and in financial trouble for years, ever since the Kennelly sons had been killed in Vietnam and their father had been thrown from a horse and broken his hip and then his heart, or maybe it was in reverse order. Mr. Kennelly had not been able to keep up his barns and horse operations properly, though once he had been famous for his class Arabians. His only stock now was a half dozen old horses of that breed which he kept and fed for sentimental reasons.

At this point, just before the Kennelly farm, the road made two deep curves, almost half of a figure eight. One could see the first curve and then, some distance ahead, the second curve, but there was an obscuring stand of roadside birches halfway in between.

It was there, at those two curves, that she thought she saw him, misted over by the light fog. He seemed to be walking on the edge of the road, ahead and away from her. If it wasn't Dallas Dobson, at least it was someone tall, in boots and a light-colored windbreaker, and there was a long, urgent lope to his stride.

She glanced at the speedometer and then slowed to a crawl, ready to honk the horn and wave, but when she looked up again, the roadside was empty.

Retta rolled down the window and continued to

drive slowly. She was puzzled, even a little upset. She had only wanted to wave. . . . Carefully, she scanned the heavy weeds in the ditches, the dewy grass along the roadside. But there was no one in sight. And no mark that she could see of muddy footprints or bruised and broken bushes where someone might have slipped off the road and hidden in the woods.

Chapter
3

Charlie Amberson, Junior, never came downstairs when her friend stopped by to pick up the newspaper column. She liked to sleep late. The Ambersons lived in a rented two-story country cottage, old and quaint. It was a red-brick structure, wreathed and vined over with decades of Virginia creeper. The creeper was green most of the year, with masses of red leaves coming in late autumn. Then, in the cold winter months, it was just a mass of bare and gnarled old vines with a few household windows peeking through. "It's like living in a damned bird's nest," young Charlotte often complained. "If I ever *do* get pregnant, I'm likely to give birth to a nestful of eggs."

The front door was unlocked as always and, as Retta pushed it open, Mrs. Amberson called out, "Just chase a cat off a chair somewhere and pour yourself some tea. I'm putting the jazz into the Kerns-Hancock wedding. Then you can dash into town and stop the presses."

Retta loved the Amberson house on these early mornings, the rooms as full of clutter and emotional turmoil as the rooms of her own house were filled with peace and caring. Retta knew that Mrs. Amberson often slept on the couch, usually in the same clothes she'd been wearing the previous evening, tossing and restless, switching at daybreak from Madeira to pots of steaming tea. She smoked brown cigarettes, holding the long, narrow cylinder in her teeth as she typed, giving her face a constant look of scorn, almost like a cynical smile.

"I'm gonna give you *heart*, Boss Caldwell," she had told Carter Caldwell when she first asked for the job. "You're from such an old, elegant family, the real elite, inherited money — what's left of it — the biggest house in the county. I don't think you know what *goes on* with everyday people out in sacred readerland. I'm going to find out and put it all down."

The column was bright, witty, and very personal. If church supper refreshments included German potato salad from a favorite grandmother's recipe, that information got into the story. If a bride sewed all six dresses for her bridesmaids, that was news. And the day Charlotte Amberson persuaded the cooks at the annual ox roast for the Po-Mar-Lin Volunteer Fire Company to give her their secret recipe for barbecue sauce, the *Zenith Press* had to print an extra edition to keep up with reader demand.

"I got a hot one today, Retta," Mrs. Amberson said that morning as she typed. "The wedding I'm writing about now — the bride met the groom on the construction site over at the new mushroom farm."

"I don't see anything very romantic about that," Retta said.

"Don't worry, I put all the romance up front." Charlotte Amberson began to read out her copy in a singsong voice. "The bride wore a satin gown made by her great-aunt Jolie Nabors, and her veil was attached to a white orchid headpiece that matched her orchid bouquet. The members of the wedding party wore silver tuxedos, with a single pink rose as boutonnieres for the best man and ushers, and a miniature white orchid for the groom."

Retta sipped her tea and smiled. "You're just making that up as you go along, aren't you?"

"Like heck I am, honey. This is *journalism*, right down to the last rum raisin in the groom's cake. And you know what the kicker is, what makes your old Aunt Char so downright readable?"

"No," Retta said.

"I found out how the lovely bride and her macho bridegroom happened to meet on that construction site. I got it typed in right between the satin ribbons on the pews and the three-tiered wedding cake. It just so happens that she's a professional plasterer,

31

and the groom had been hired on as an assistant lather. She was the boss! Now that's modern, that's *today*."

Mrs. Amberson sighed, snuffed out her cigarette, folded her typed sheets neatly, and slipped them into an envelope. She handed it to Retta. "There you are, cupcake. I wish it were coverage of the United Nations, but at least I'm working up to my talents. And I do get better readership than your mother with her do-gooder editorials."

Retta had heard this strain of teasing jealousy before, so she said simply, "Well, Mother's been doing those editorials for only about three years, since Two and I grew up, and I think she's very good at it."

Mrs. Amberson sighed. "Of course she is. She's a fine writer and I'm just mad that I can't write that way. But she'll never stop that bypass highway from going right through this part of the countryside. And I don't have to read my tarot cards to know that."

"Nothing's definite," Retta said. "The *Zenith Press* just wants its readers to know the law, and to be informed of their options."

"Spoken like a real Caldwell," Mrs. Amberson said. "Boring, but true." And then she stopped. "Pretend I didn't say that, Retta. I'd be a lost soul if your father hadn't hired me, and if you didn't drive my copy into town each day."

"I love to do it," Henrietta said. "It's a kind of training for me and it helps earn my allowance."

Mrs. Amberson lit another cigarette and ran a nervous hand through her hair. "You know I can drive perfectly well, and have for years, but I can't face the big world out there until three o'clock. I can't calm down. I tried to talk the whole thing out with a psychiatrist in West Chester. He wanted to tie it in with religious guilt. I used to be a church-goer, you know. This well-meaning shrink asked me if I thought my 'three o'clock problem' had anything to do with the fact that Christ was crucified two thousand years ago at exactly three o'clock." She laughed without humor. "I told him I didn't operate on Jerusalem time, and he told me to find another doctor. He didn't treat jokers."

Retta was aware that Mrs. Amberson was tense, anxious, stalling for time, trying as always to prolong these moments of conversation that kept her in touch with youth and the outside world, two things she had begun to fear. "Mrs. Amberson," Retta said gently, "we're both on deadline. If I don't get this material into Zenith right away, I'll be late for my eight o'clock class."

"Okay, okay," the older woman said, walking toward the front door. "But by the way, I'd like to know how you think my little Charlotte is getting along these days. I see more of you than I do of her, you know. She's always taking those long walks of hers and hiding up in her room the rest of the time. How's she doing in school? She hardly ever tells me anything. But I can trust you, can't I, Retta? You'd tell me, wouldn't you, if she were into drugs or anything, or if she and some boy were messing around? You'll be honest with me about Charlie, won't you?" She put a rough, restraining hand on

Retta's arm. "If you weren't, I think I'd kick your aristocratic little butt right out the front door of Tara here. . . ."

Henrietta felt a knot of sudden and intense anger in her chest, and her cheeks were hot. "Mrs. Amberson," she said, trying to keep the tears out of her voice, "I simply do not understand you or people like you. You are speaking of someone I love and respect, my very best friend. How can you do this?"

Mrs. Amberson was instantly contrite, her eyes moist and shining. "Oh, Henrietta, where's your compassion? You've got to let a neurotic old shut-in talk like this once in a while. Young Charlotte is all I've got and — "

"And that's an even worse thing to say," Retta cut in. "You can't claim you've 'got' Charlotte, like she's something you *own*. Parents can love children and enjoy them, but they don't *own* them like they're little birds in a cage with a lock. And how about you, Mrs. Amberson? Don't you 'own' yourself? You're supposed to make *yourself* count in life. . . ."

Though most of the morning fog had burned away, Retta warned herself to drive with extra care. Twice in one morning, her emotions had veered off center.

It was almost twenty minutes to eight when she reached the newspaper offices, still shuttered and locked for the night, and slipped the Amberson copy through a slot in the front door. Soon the whole county would know about the silver tuxedos and the rum raisins in the groom's cake, and everything else, she thought grimly.

The final eight o'clock bell rang just as Henrietta opened the door of the math classroom. With a quick nod of apology to Mr. Engel, she hurried to her desk. Her thoughts were still far outside the classroom. *What's happening to me?* she thought. *When did life stop being easy to handle? When did so many things cease to be simple and dependable?*

Her pencil dropped from the spine of her notebook and rolled into the aisle, just behind her. As she bent to pick it up, she realized Dallas Dobson was already in his seat. She turned and glanced at him quickly. His face was intent and impersonal, eyes looking straight ahead. But there was no fog in this classroom. She had not imagined it. He *was* wearing a windbreaker, light-colored, not white exactly, but a faded beige.

Both Caldwell students brought parental notes to school the next day, asking to be excused from afternoon classes. Henrietta ate an apple as she drove home and, when she got there, her parents and brother were waiting in the station wagon at the end of the lane. She parked her car at the gate and joined them.

The town meeting was scheduled for one o'clock in a second-floor conference room at the Zenith bank. It was an all-beige room, with beige rugs, beige draperies, and three rows of folding chairs, cushioned in beige. There was a large map propped on an easel stand, a speakers' table with five chairs, and a hand microphone. Behind that a wall of blown-up photographs were pinned side by side across the span of the room.

"It's a pro and con meeting," Mrs. Caldwell had explained on the drive to town, "a place for concerned citizens to speak out. If either of you has anything to say — say it. Otherwise, just sit up tall and look damned mad about the whole thing."

There were about twenty people in the folding chairs, and two men behind the table with the microphone. Since their faces were unfamiliar, Henrietta guessed they would speak for the Zenith bypass and the highway planners in Harrisburg. In the second row of chairs, Retta recognized two librarians, a clerk from the state liquor store, the Zale brothers from the appliance shop, and Mr. Berk who owned Towne Fashions.

Hugo Provanza sat in the front row. Retta recognized him, not from his burly shoulders or bald head, but because he was wearing a Havendale High football jacket with Junior Provanza's number on it. Mr. Provanza had left school in the seventh grade but was a regular rooter at all Havendale sporting events.

Just outside the beige-draped windows, the mounted bank clock ticked loudly, a reverberation like a sharp hiccup running through the tension of the meeting room. At a quarter past one, Carter Caldwell said to the men at the speakers' table, "Gentlemen, I think everyone who plans to attend is now here."

It was a Mr. Burt Myerson who stood up, introduced himself, and said he spoke on behalf of Harrisburg. With a yardstick, he traced the route of the proposed highway on the easeled map, explaining in some detail the current traffic statistics and then the increased number of vehicles that would be attracted by the new bypass.

"What we propose to do," he said, "is to facilitate the passage of traffic on this new interstate highway and lift the burden of transport that is now streaming through and jamming up your town, the town of Zenith."

The older Zale brother raised his hand, like a child in school, and said loudly, "You seem to forget that *some* of the traffic is driving into Zenith to shop there. We *need* those customers."

"I think you will get *more* customers," Mr. Myerson said smoothly, "if your town becomes more *attractive* to shoppers, if we can *lighten* the traffic load now on your narrow main thoroughfare and the side streets."

One of the librarians rose to her feet and addressed both Mr. Myerson and the room in general. "You're not listening to your own words, sir," she said firmly. "And unless we're speaking different languages, your proposed plan will induce customers *to forget* about Zenith and drive to shopping malls in bigger towns. Isn't that what the term 'bypass' means? That the town of Zenith and its inhabitants and merchants will be *passed by*?"

A flutter of applause swept the room. Mrs. Caldwell was taking notes while Carter Caldwell was frowning at the eight-foot panorama of photographs on the wall. Retta and Two were clapping with the others.

For the next forty minutes, there were discussions back and forth between the townspeople and the men from Harrisburg. For every citizen argument against the new highway, Mr. Myerson had an answer, a list of statistics, or a demonstration graph to show economic growth in other towns involved in bypass situations. To Retta, the man seemed falsely cheerful, almost as if he were humoring little children.

At exactly two o'clock, Burt Myerson pushed aside his chair again and walked to the enlarged pictures. "Here," he said, "we have a photographic blowup of the entire farm and residential area outside Zenith that will be affected by construction. If you will compare the route on the map with the photographs, you will see that we have laid out the new highway to spare as many homes, businesses, and farm buildings as possible." He waved his hand to indicate on the photographs where the bypass might go. "I think our planners did very well indeed."

"Your plan says you're not going to *knock down* any of my buildings," Hugo Provanza interrupted, "but you cut me in half. I'll end up with my general store on one side of a six-lane highway and my house on the other."

Carter Caldwell got to his feet without a word and stepped close to the panoramic photographs, tracing carefully over the black and white surface with the index finger of his right hand. Retta noticed that his other hand was behind him, clenched so tightly that the knuckles flinched white.

When he spoke, his voice was deliberately calm and unemotional. "Mr. Myerson," he said, "your planners did so well that they have eliminated our house and outbuildings entirely. Our structures do not show on these photographs, nor are they sketched on your map."

"Oh?" Mr. Myerson said. "The map was drawn *from* the photographs. Just where is your place?"

"Your proposed highway passes south of us, through both fields and meadowlands, and our home is right here." Caldwell put his hand, fingers outspread, directly over a large, dark clump of trees in the photographic blowup.

"I see. That's an oversight, but a correctable one," the man said smoothly. "I'll have an engineer stop by your place to get an idea of mass and measurements. Then we can put you on the map. You see, our team took these aerial photographs at a considerable height and with a telescopic lens. They didn't penetrate your heavy cover of trees."

Retta listened to the man's easy words and felt emotion rush through her till her lips were stiff and numb, as if sucked dry by a sudden fear. They had been secretly spied on, a plane right over their own house, but high, so high that they could neither see nor hear it. When had that tiny silver cross droned through the sky, taking these terrible pictures? What had they all been doing then, so unaware that overhead a powerful camera was determining the fate of their beloved Springhill?

"We might be doing you a favor," Mr. Myerson said, "by thinning out your timber when we build the bypass through your property. You seem to have an oversupply of shade around your house."

"You wouldn't *dare* do that," Two Caldwell said, his voice shocked. "Some of those trees are William Penn oaks, planted more than two hundred years ago. My father's family has always lived there. We love those trees. . . ." Casually, Mrs. Caldwell lifted an arm and put it around the back of her son's chair.

" 'Dare' isn't a word we need in our vocabulary at the highway department," Mr. Myerson said. "Not when we have the law on our side, the statute of 'Right of Eminent Domain.' That law gives the commonwealth the right to decide what's best for the majority of the people." He paused. "Each landowner affected by our plans has a right to hire a lawyer to examine his case. Or he can put his pros and cons on paper for my department. We are still in the discussion stage, hence this meeting. We are still open to suggestions."

"But you just said '*when* we build the bypass through your property,' " Two protested.

"A manner of speaking, sonny," Myerson said, gathering together his sheaf of papers. "Just a manner of speaking. We're still flexible. And the state will compensate all owners for land confiscated at the going rate for real estate, the price to be decided on. We'll try to be fair," he said, looking impassively at the group and then more pointedly at Two. "But remember, we can't pay you for your memories. Or your dreams."

40

Chapter
4

Henrietta Caldwell had always believed a touch of melancholy could add to the pleasure of life, that a temporary background of gray moods could hype the lighter tones, bring out the brightness in everyday things. Yet she could not understand the strange new sadness underlying her thoughts for most of the week, since the morning after her harsh words with Mrs. Amberson. It could have been that incident, she knew. Or it might stem from something else.

But the next day, and the next and the next, there had been no blue cigarette smoke, no offers of sweet tea while Charlotte's mother typed out the last paragraphs of her newspaper copy. No, each morning now, a completed column was left on the front porch, held down against stray winds by a potted aster plant tinted with the purple and red colors of autumn.

Behind the front door, Mrs. Amberson must be sulking, or perhaps she felt sad, too, Retta thought. *Or maybe she's waiting to see if I would be foolish enough to tell Charlotte what she said.*

Now the columns were dropped off at the *Zenith Press* each morning a full half hour ahead of schedule. That gave Retta extra time to follow a different route to school each day as she wished. But for the past few mornings she had, without wondering why, chosen the two-lane country road that curved past the Kennelly property and the big, sagging horse barn.

Fall that year was touched with Indian summer. On each side of the road tall clumps of goldenrod grew four feet tall, the flowering clusters heavy with pollen and dust from the road. Retta was acutely aware of the beauty of these autumn mornings, the isolation of the back roads, the movement and color of the flowers, the tiny rhythmic sting of sound as bits of gravel spun up from the roadway and hit the side of the car. It seemed to her that her senses, her appreciation, her longings had reached a peak of intensity that she had rarely been aware of before.

This morning she drove more slowly than usual, then pulled to the side of the road and brought the car to a stop to watch a giant Monarch butterfly, its wings a mesh of black and orange. It drifted across the road and settled on a wand of goldenrod, the color of its frail wings almost blending into the dusty yellow flower. Retta watched, almost without thought, caught up in the delicate magic of the moment.

Suddenly, with no warning, someone stepped out from a clump of sumac bush and slammed a hand on the hood of the car. The voice was cold, touched with deep anger, as Dallas Dobson said, "All right, Miss Caldwell. I have had just about enough of this. Tell me why you have been following me."

For a moment, she was stunned into silence, then opened the car door and stepped out. She wanted to be standing herself when she talked to this tall, hostile stranger. Though she had seen him every day in school for nearly two weeks, this was the first time they had spoken.

"Following you? *Me* following *you*, Dallas Dobson? This is my road, too, you know. I *live* near here. This is the way I drive to school."

"You don't always come this way," he said. "Monday was the first day I saw you. I ditched you that time."

"Then you *were* walking along the road that morning. There was that fog — " Retta stopped sharply, then said, "And why are *you* keeping track of *me*, may I ask? Why did you duck out of sight when I came around the curve that morning?"

The tall boy took his hand off the hood and jammed it deep in his jeans pocket. "I didn't want you to see me. I don't want people feeling sorry for me," he said.

"Do you *live* here? What are you talking about?"

Dobson shrugged. "I'm not from this neighborhood. Old Mr. Kennelly and his wife live here. Alone.

I hired on to groom and service the six horses. They're old but they're good Arabian stock. I feed them, exercise them a little, and muck out the stables every morning early, seven days a week. The job pays, and on weekends I can ride them if I want to."

"But why are you angry with me? Didn't you want me to see you walking? Are you ashamed just because you don't have a car? Lots of people — "

"We have a car," he said. "A pickup. But I have to leave it for my dad. He's a cripple now, you know."

"How would I ever know that?" she said.

He shrugged again and kicked at the graveled road with his Texas boot. "It's such a big thing in our lives, I just presumed everybody 'round here had heard about the accident.

"Here's how it is," he said, looking straight at her for the first time. "I've been hitching a ride over here mornings, with a milk truck. Then I walk over to the main road to get a hitch to school. I thought you were trying to track me. Something to tell your friends about. I thought you wanted to be sorry for me."

The butterfly lifted itself from the goldenrod and the stalk bounced up gently, sending a dust of pollen onto the ground. They watched as it drifted to the other side of the road and then out of sight.

"As a little kid in Texas, I used to want to catch those things," Dobson said, "but my brother explained that if you touch a butterfly's wings, well, they're so delicate, it can never fly again."

Henrietta looked at her watch. "Your brother's

right, I guess. But we've got other problems. We'll be late for class. Don't argue with me. Just get in. I'm giving you a lift."

Retta took off down the road with a little squeal of gravel. Dobson sat in the passenger seat, his knees touching the dashboard, his head just inches from the sunroof. The girl glanced at him and noticed his hands: big, brown, folded quietly on one knee. He caught her glance, then turned casually to crank down his window.

"That will make it better," he said.

"What do you mean?" she said.

"Fresh air. I've got special permission to shower in the men's locker room. If I'm late, I just skip the first class."

"That isn't what I was thinking at all," she said vehemently. "Lots of people at Havendale smell of horses. It's a good smell. Take the Drexel brothers, for instance. They ride to school every morning if the weather's good. They like to smell like horses. . . ."

Dallas laughed softly. "Gentleman's manure. There's a big difference. They ride it; I shovel it."

He asked to be let off near the rear door to the gym, and when she stopped the car, Retta said, "Look, I can give you a lift any day. If you're at the Kennelly gate, you ride."

He was thoughtful a moment, then said, "Miss Caldwell, I don't want to get you in trouble with your parents. Maybe they wouldn't like you doing favors for Dallas Dobson."

"It's just hitchhikers they worry about," Retta said

quickly. "You're a fellow student, after all. And my parents aren't like that, anyway. You'll see when you meet them sometime."

"Meet them? Thanks, but I don't think I ever will," he said, and set off in a brisk run toward the school building.

"Monday," she called after him. "I mean it, Monday morning. . . ."

But she could not tell whether Dallas Dobson had heard her or not.

That evening, her father called to say he would be held up at the office till seven-thirty. Two ate his dinner on a tray in front of the TV, but Mrs. Caldwell put the salad in the refrigerator and three dinner plates in a low oven. She and Retta waited.

When Carter Caldwell did come home, he and his wife seated themselves at the table while Retta went to the kitchen for salad and warm food.

As she pushed her way through the swinging door, she heard her father say, "We just don't know yet. All the figures aren't in. So far, we're no worse off than we were last month, but no better off, either. It's just too early to tell."

"Retta, go to the cabinet and bring your father a glass of red wine, will you? He's had a hard day."

Retta poured a glass of Bordeaux into an old stemmed goblet and set it on her father's placemat. Then she poured a second goblet for her mother. She looked at both parents, aware of their thoughtful silence, the worried concern on their faces. At that moment she knew they were not so much caring parents as two separate and adult people, preoccupied with their own problems.

Maybe later, she thought. She had meant to tell the family, at dinner, all about meeting Dallas Dobson. Yet either the matter wasn't important *enough* to bring up or it was *too* important. Retta wasn't sure. But she decided that this was not the right moment to mention her arrangement with the new boy at school.

Chapter
5

The first week was uneventful. For three straight days, Retta picked up Dallas Dobson at the end of the Kennelly lane, then dropped him off at the entrance to the school drive so he could sprint back to the showers. It was an association both constrained and polite: a few words each day, a smile of thanks. Nothing more.

On Friday, she put a Willie Nelson medley in the tape deck and listened as she drove to the Kennellys'. Dobson smiled as he got in the car, then picked up the lyrics to "Sunday Mornin' Comin' Down" in a soft, rich tenor, with a distinct Texas twang. He drummed his long, hard fingers against the dashboard, almost as if he were playing background guitar.

Just before he got out of the car at the school gate, he said lightly, "I know you picked Willie Nelson for me, the good-ole-boy stuff. How about I provide the music next week? I've got an early tape of Duke Ellington doing jazz. It's old but still good. . . ."

"I like Ellington," she said, feeling a flush of embarrassment touch her cheeks. "But I wasn't thinking of good ole boys. Willie Nelson is a favorite of *mine*, too."

"A little of each," he said. "We'll balance out. A little of each."

But on Monday he was not at the Kennellys' gate nor in math class, either. Not till Thursday was he there, and Retta guessed by the agitated way he was pacing the gravel lane that he had forgotten about the Ellington tape.

As he swung into the car, he said abruptly, "My father was kind of sick and I had to take his place at work."

"Sick?" she said. "What does the doctor say?"

"Nothing," Dobson said. "It isn't that kind of sickness."

He took a math book out of his jacket pocket and leafed through the pages to the right place. "I've been on the double," he said, "working the Kennelly chores early so I could get to the feed store on time." His voice sounded tense, impatient. "First I lose two years at school after my father's accident. And now

I lose three days out of a single week. I'm not sure I can catch up."

"You could have called me," she said, "to tell me you wouldn't need a lift. I waited each morning."

"Call you?" he said, and his tone was guarded and impersonal. He flipped a page in the math book to a new lesson. "I didn't think that was necessary, or that it was something you'd want me to do."

They drove on in silence. Dobson held the math book in one hand, his eyes narrowed, his lips moving slightly as he concentrated on the equations. His left hand lay in repose on his knee. Suddenly, she noticed a deep, livid scratch reaching from his thumb, over the back of his hand, and up into the sleeve of his jacket.

She heard her own quick, involuntary intake of breath and reached out to touch his hand. "You're hurt," she said. "How did you get a scratch like that?"

He did not take his eyes off the book as he spoke. "A barn cat," he said simply. "I was forking in hay and got too near her hideaway. She's got kittens in there. She jumped out and gave me a warning."

"It's so deep," she said, her fingers still resting lightly on his hand. "It could get infected. . . ."

"I'll clean it in the shower," he said.

"I don't believe in barn cats, even if they do keep the mice down," she said. "It isn't fair to turn a tame cat into a feral one. Couldn't you give it a little milk once in a while? Couldn't you try that?"

He didn't answer, but when she had pulled into the school drive and stopped, he said, "Thanks.

Thanks for picking me up today." He opened the car door. "And let's not worry about that barn cat, Retta. It's between her and me. Some things just don't want to be tamed, you know."

As he jogged up the driveway, Retta saw Junior Provanza hail him and then walk toward him with his twin sister, Parma, and a female cousin she knew was visiting the Provanzas.

Dobson waited till the trio caught up with him and together they walked toward the rear doors of the school.

Retta felt a stab of emotion so unexpected that she had to grip the steering wheel to bring it under control. Besides taking Mr. Engel's math class together and their almost silent morning rides, she never saw Dallas Dobson, did not know where he lived, or what he did with his spare time. She was experiencing something irrational and unwelcome. It was the emotional discomfort of simple jealousy. She did not know he had made other friends.

Fall weather doesn't turn into winter in Pennsylvania until the rainy winds of November pound the last leaves from the trees and blow ice crusts over the morning dews. This year even the rains were late. Bright fall leaves, a fiery red and gold, stayed until almost Thanksgiving. Then, after three days of gray, misting downpour, the winds cleared the trees so completely that bare branches were like black etchings against the sky.

It was a bittersweet time for the Caldwells. Without the autumn flowers and brightly colored leaves to add a mood of carnival to the countryside, the red flags in the route of the new highway stood out brighter than ever, unfaded by winds or rain.

Sometimes Dallas was waiting at the Kennellys' gate five days in a week. Then for two weeks in a row he might be there only Thursday and Friday. On the rides to school, he rarely spoke, frowning over the pages of the math book, drumming his fingers restlessly on the red leather dashboard.

One day he did bring an Ellington tape. He slid down deep in the car seat, both hands cupped behind his head as he listened with closed eyes, humming along softly with the violins in "Blues in C." "It belonged to my brother," was all he said.

Next morning, Retta slipped the cassette into the tape deck just as she pulled away from the offices of the *Zenith Press*. When she sighted him waiting at the Kennelly gate, she rolled down her window and let the sweet, sophisticated music sound out into the cold morning air.

He smiled at her as he got into the car, a quick, grateful smile, almost shy. "I wasn't sure you liked it," he said. "It tells me something about you, Retta. Something I like a lot."

And those were the only words they exchanged that late fall morning.

Since Charlotte Amberson did not drive, the two friends met at the Amberson house when they needed to study together. It was a natural exchange. Charlotte helped Retta out with a half hour of Spanish conversation (the Ambersons had lived in Puerto

Rico, attached to the state department, before the last divorce) and Retta paid off with an hour of intense tutoring in math. It was usually not more than ten in the evening when she turned her car into her own driveway.

It was Charlotte's idea to have Dallas Dobson join them. Mrs. Amberson had silently apologized to Retta for asking her about Charlie by greeting her one morning with a finished column and a light kiss.

"The cowboy's worse off than I am," Charlie had said. "At least I know I hate all forms of math and I don't plan to go to college anyway, unless Mother makes a big fuss. But he's a high-I.Q. type and he's still going to flunk that class if somebody doesn't help him."

Only that morning she had sat in class, apprehensive and oddly ashamed, trying not to listen as Dallas stumbled wildly when called on for an answer. He finally had to give up. When Mr. Engel called on Retta next, she told him deliberately that she hadn't been able to understand that problem, either. Mr. Engel looked puzzled, then put a red check next to CALDWELL in his grades book.

On the first night the three studied together, Mrs. Amberson put her head into the door of the small study. She was bright-eyed and alert, fruity with the smell of Madeira and brown cigarettes. When Charlotte introduced Dobson, the older woman shook his hand and then whispered, as if to herself, "Gad, what a hunk."

"Don't mind my mother," Charlie said when the door closed. "She gets all her witty lines from late movies on TV." But Retta saw her friend's eyes were bright with tears.

It was a Thursday night in late November when Charlie called during the dinner hour and Retta excused herself to take the call.

"It's a message from Billy the Kid," she said crisply. "He'll be waiting in front of the Provanza market around seven-thirty tonight. He can hitch that far. His daddy took the pickup truck to visit a lady, and Billy needs transportation."

"You don't have to talk to me in code," Retta said sharply.

"I wasn't sure if Dallas Dobson is a welcome name at your house," Charlotte said.

"I don't know why you'd say that," Retta said.

"Hey! This is your best friend you're talking to, Miss Caldwell," Charlotte said. "I notice you never invite him over to your house to study."

It was a quarter to ten and the trio still had three pages to review when Dobson closed his book and said, "I think I've learned all I can for one evening."

"But the test's on Monday and you have to work most of the weekend," Retta said.

"Let *me* worry about that," he said. "At least I know more now than I did a month ago."

But at the Ambersons' gate, Dallas Dobson put his hand on the steering wheel, almost as if he wanted to stop the car. Then he said quietly, "It's still early, Retta. Can't we go somewhere? There are things I want to tell you."

Retta felt her heartbeat quicken, a rapid, erratic rhythm, almost as if she were frightened. "The Dairy Queen Drive-In closes at ten," she said lightly. "And except for bars, there's nothing still open in Zenith."

Suddenly, she was acutely aware of something she had forgotten for months. The key was still in her red handbag, now on the backseat. An almost involuntary memory of Aunt Blue's house flashed through her mind: the silence; the privacy; the front room with the long, red couch with lace doilies on the arms; the birch logs and kindling in the fireplace, ready for a match. No one would ever need to know. . . .

She paused and looked at the young man beside her, his face thoughtful in profile, the only sound in the car the warm, even cadence of his breathing.

She ran the tip of her tongue over her dry, cool lips and then willed herself to say, "I can't think of anywhere to go around here this time of night, Dallas. It's all just small-town."

"There are things I've been thinking about that I wanted to tell you," he said again.

"If you don't mind just sitting in the car, we can always park over on the Kennelly road," she said, "There's never any traffic there this time of night."

He nodded and Retta backed carefully into the Ambersons' gravel drive, then pulled forward and made a sharp right. If Mrs. Amberson was watching from an upstairs window — and Retta had the feeling she was — she would know that they were not driving straight home.

She rolled the window halfway down on her side

of the car, and felt the cool night air touch her face. The Kennelly house, with a single light on the second floor, was just around the bend, and she could hear the whisper of night wind in the trees and the almost silent sounds of birds and animals moving in the darkness. The breeze had the damp, green smell of lichen and mosses, touched with the dusty sweetness of goldenrod. Dallas put his arm around the back of her car seat, not touching her, but close enough so she could smell the scent of saddle soap and feel the faint heat from his hand.

"Maybe you don't even want to hear what I have to say," he began. "If you want me to stop, if you want to start the car and drive on home, just say so. I'll understand. Believe me, I'll understand, Retta. I don't want to come on too strong. I don't want to put you under any obligation to hear me out if that's something you'd rather not do. . . ."

He stopped, staring out thoughtfully through the dark windshield, almost as if he were not sure how to go on.

"Please," she said softly. "Please say what you want to say."

He took a deep breath, closed his eyes tightly for a moment, then opened them. She waited, then turned to face him directly. "Please. I mean it. It must be important, what you're thinking about."

"All right," he said abruptly. "It's just this, Henrietta. I think we are going to be more than friends. So there are things you should know about me, things I want to tell you myself."

Chapter
6

She said nothing, waiting, and when he spoke again his voice was calm and under control, as if he had thought about these words a long time.

"I know you are Henrietta Caldwell, and all that goes with that. One day, right after we got here, my father drove his pickup past your house and told me, 'That's where the Caldwells live.'

"I'm Dallas Dobson, a kid out of Texas. I know who my father is. I live with him. But he never married my mother, or my brother's mother, either. Technically, Dallas Dobson is a bastard."

He touched the back of her hair lightly, fingering the softness of the little half-moon curls.

"My brother's mother was a girl from Zenith. I

never knew her. When she got pregnant right out of high school, my father ran away with her to Texas. He did the thing he liked to do best — bumming around the rodeos, taking care of stock for eating money, and picking up prize cash when he could. My father was one hell of a rider before the accident. As a kid, he was a great ice-skater, too. We didn't see any of that in Texas, but he told me about it. Anyway, that first lady left him after about four years, and he kept the little boy. He was my brother. Sam Houston Dobson was what they called him.

"They lived in trailers, ranch bunkhouses, motel rooms, even the back of pickup trucks. Sometimes Sam Houston got to school, sometimes he didn't. But he was one of the best trick riders in the Southwest. Anyone would tell you that."

He laughed. "Once, when Sam Houston was only eighteen, my father took him and me to Hawaii for the start of the rodeo season."

"I'd never think there were rodeos in Hawaii," Retta said.

"There are. Most of the big-timers skip them, but there's good prize money. Sam Houston won a saddle worth nearly five hundred bucks."

"That must have made your father very proud."

Dallas shrugged. "Maybe, but father had hoped the two of them would win more. We had to sell that saddle to fly back to the mainland."

"And you? What about you, Dallas?" Retta asked softly.

"I'm a different case," he said. "My brother was six years older than me. And my mother, the girl

58

that had me, was just a kid, just turned seventeen, my father told me. She'd lied about her age and got a job with a traveling rodeo as a back-up clown. They played San Antonio one summer and my father signed up with them for a while. That's when they got to know each other.

"My father told me my mother wore a big red and white clown suit with a yellow wig and turned-up shoes. She painted red circles on her cheeks, he told me, and drew big black eyelashes on her face so she looked crazy, but all beautiful at the same time. If a rider gets tossed or is hurt, it's the clown's job to run into the ring and shout and swing a big cape to lure the steer or the bronc in another direction. They dress and *act* like clowns, but they are more like animal trainers and they have to be quick and brave. A lot depends on them.

"My mother was the best, my father told me. Once he was thrown by a big pinto, and she ran out and grabbed the bridle so my father didn't get stomped to death." His voice was suddenly warm with affection and pride. "You know, because of her build and that baggy clown suit, people didn't even guess she was pregnant. I was out there with her, right into her seventh month."

"But she and your father never got married?"

"No," he said flatly. "My father didn't want to, I'm sure of that, and my mother — well, she was just a kid, you know. She had her baby in a neighborhood clinic down in Waco and planned to give it away to a rich family with no children, but my father wouldn't let her." He was silent for a long beat and then said, "My father wanted me and he got me. We've been together ever since."

"And your brother Sam Houston?"

This time the silence was so deep, so pronounced, that Retta wondered if he had heard her at all. Then he spoke quietly, almost in a hoarse whisper. "This hurts me to talk about, Retta. It's something I've been having trouble with for nearly three years. Sam Houston is dead. He and my father were coming home by motorcycle one night after a big bash at some buddy's ranch. The cycle went off the road and hit a tree. When the highway cops got there, they were both lying on the ground. Sam Houston was dead and my father had his right leg shattered right from the ankle up through the hip. And he was bruised and unconscious because his head hit that tree. It was three days before he could tell anyone what happened."

"What did happen?"

"Well, I can't blame him for it, really, he had enough troubles. My father told the cops that Sam Houston was driving."

"And you don't believe that?"

"Put it this way, Retta. My brother wasn't a drinker and my father was. He's been a womanizer and party man as long as I can remember. It's just the way he is. But he can't force himself to remember or, at least, admit who hit the gas that night. Lately, when he's really drinking, I can tell he wants to tell me something — but just can't. Sam Houston was his favorite. Maybe he doesn't want me to hear the truth.

"After the accident, I just dropped out of school for two years to take care of my dad. He had a lot of pain and nobody but me to help him. I bagged groceries at supermarkets, for a while I had part-time work on a peanut farm, and weekends I hustled any kind of horse job. We were drifters. There was no one to notice whether Dallas Dobson was in school or not. So Havendale High is like a last chance for me."

"But why not in Texas? Why in this part of Pennsylvania?"

Dallas shrugged. "Just as soon as he was well enough to get around on crutches, my father started to say he wanted to go home. He was born in Zenith, you know. His mother and father were kind of old and they're gone now. My father was an only child. His parents rented one of those row houses behind the state liquor store." He laughed abruptly. "If you know that section of town, that tells you something about the Dobson family tree."

As Dallas talked, Henrietta heard every word he said, but she was also listening to the profound silence that surrounded them. It was a night with stars but no moon, and the trees and heavy growth along the roadside were only dim shapes, black on black. The wind sounds were light, rhythmic, and distant, while the inside of the small car seemed to echo with memories of the Ellington music.

Henrietta's thoughts seemed as loud in her mind as spoken words. *How can I be sure this is real? How can I believe that it is truly me sitting in the darkness, listening to a stranger tell me faraway*

61

things about himself? It is almost as if I have stopped being Henrietta Caldwell and have become someone else. Except for this person sitting next to me, no one in the entire world knows where I am right now. Not my parents, not Charlotte, not Aunt Blue. . . .

"I needed to tell you because I never want you to feel sorry for me," Dallas Dobson was saying. "It isn't as if my mother just *gave* me away. My father *is* my father and she knew he wanted me." He paused. "Maybe you'll think this is just another tall story for him to tell me, but I believe it.

"My mother's married now," he went on. "She lives in some little town in Texas, with a good husband and a pair of twin girls. But she wanted me to know who and where she was, my father says. So I can find her anytime I want to. He has her married name and address on a card in his wallet. I just have to ask for it."

"Are you going to?" Retta said. "Is that what you plan to do?"

He shook his head. "I don't think so. I used to dream about it, but not now. Without Sam Houston, and with my father crippled and all, maybe I don't need a mother anymore."

Suddenly his voice lowered, the sentence trailing off almost to a whisper. Retta leaned toward him to catch his words, her cheek almost touching his.

"I only miss my mother sometimes now," he said softly. "Like on holidays, when other people have families. Or when I see a sweater or some kind of necklace in a store and I think how much I'd like to buy it for her. She probably thinks of buying things for me sometimes. Just a young kid, she was. She must wonder about me sometimes, certainly every time my birthday rolls 'round."

"A baby," Retta whispered. "I think she probably thinks of you mostly as a baby, almost like when she saw you last."

"She only kept me with her in the clinic a few hours," he said. "I used to imagine that if she *had* stayed with us, she'd have called me. . . ." He paused.

"Called you what?" Retta said.

His words were barely audible now. ". . . she'd have called me 'Little Cowboy' or something." He took his arm from around Retta's shoulders and rubbed the dark windshield with the back of his hand.

"What's the matter?" Retta asked. "What are you looking at?"

"I don't know," he whispered, then put a finger to his lips. "Quiet a moment," he said, and listened intently. Then he frowned. "What could it be? I hear movement, Henrietta. I've heard it twice now. Don't you hear something? There's someone or something out there."

Retta listened, staring at the black windshield and the black road beyond. When she held her breath so the silence in the car would be complete, she was aware of the quickening beat of her heart. Still she heard nothing.

Carefully Dallas rolled down his window and waited, listening to the dark, leafy stillness of the night. "Turn on your parking lights," he whispered.

The soft lights prodded the nearby darkness, but lit nothing but a stretch of gravel and roadside weeds. "Now your headlights," he said quietly.

She turned the lights to bright. They both gasped at what they saw. First just a pair of eyes, gleaming red in the car lights, and then the outlines of a small, gray fox, standing motionless directly ahead of them in the road.

"He must be sick or hurt," Dallas said. "Otherwise he'd make for cover. I'm going to look at him." He stepped from the car, his movements slow and easy, and walked toward the little fox.

Retta stepped from her side of the car and followed. "He's shivering. He's cold or *something*," she whispered.

Without warning, like a toy collapsing, the fox dropped down to the roadway, hind legs stretched out, small muzzle resting on its front paws. In the headlights, they could make out its coloring: gray and buff with black markings on the ear tips and long tail. The animal was panting, the narrow red tongue coated and dry.

"Young," Dobson said. "No more than a few months. Foxes 'round here kit in springtime. He's too young to fend for himself." He bent down and cautiously touched the black, leathery tip of the fox's nose. "Hot," he said, "like a sick baby."

Putting one big hand on the animal's skull, just behind the ears, he held it immobile while he felt first the hind and then the forelegs for breaks or other injury. "He's got to be sick. Probably wandered off from a den near here. No healthy fox would tolerate humans touching him this way."

"We can't just leave it," Retta said. "He could die here or be hit by a car." Dallas slipped off his windbreaker and put it over the young fox like a blanket. "Let's take him to my house," she said. "My father will know what to do."

The young man lifted the fox carefully with the windbreaker tight around the body to hold the legs firmly trussed. "I don't want him scratching or biting from fright," he said.

The fox looked at them with sharp, vulpine eyes, dimmed a little by fever, and made no attempt to escape.

The car tires spun briefly on the loose gravel as Retta turned the car around, then tractioned into speed as she maneuvered the curves of the country lanes leading to the Caldwell house.

"Home, baby," he said softly to the animal. "Retta's gonna take you home."

When she came downstairs and stepped outside again, he was just where she'd left him, standing by the back door, cradling the fox in his arms like a human infant. The big house was dark except for one upstairs light which shone dimly, laying a precise white rectangle on the cold ground.

"What did your father say?"

Henrietta hesitated. She had rushed upstairs to her parents' room, knocked lightly, then called through the closed door, "Wake up, Poppy. We've got a sick fox outside. What should we do?"

There was no answer. Both parents were as silent

as if they were asleep, yet Retta sensed movement somewhere in the bedroom. "Pops," she whispered again. "A sick fox . . . what shall we do?"

Then she thought she heard the sound of her father's voice, soft, almost muffled. Perhaps he had said, "Tomorrow, Retta." Perhaps he had said something else. She did not know. Gently, she turned the knob and put her shoulder against the door. It did not move. She realized then that her parents' door was locked from the inside.

"What did he say we should do?" he asked again.

"Nothing," Retta said. "I didn't want to wake them."

"All right," Dobson said. "Here's what we'll need: a couple of big bath towels and something like a laundry basket to put him in."

"I can get all that," Retta said.

"And a cup of warm milk — just warm, not hot — about three tablespoons of brandy, and a couple of aspirin."

"Will you come inside and help me?" she asked.

"No," he said quietly. "I'll just wait for you here."

She brought out the basket and towels first, then heated the milk and poured it into a small Gorham pitcher from the silver coffee set. There was a bottle of aspirin in the downstairs bathroom, brandy in the liquor cabinet.

Outside, Dallas sat cross-legged on the ground; the fox, wrapped in a towel, immobile in the crook of his arm. With his free hand, he crumbled two aspirin into the milk and added a splash of brandy, stirring the mixture with his finger.

"Too hot," he said softly. "We'll let it cool for a

minute or two." Retta knelt on the ground beside him, cradling the little silver pitcher in her hands. She was aware of the rhythmic panting of the little fox, so ill, so docile, and yet so pulsing with life.

Dallas shifted the animal until he had it grasped firmly but safely between his knees. Again he tested the milk with a finger, then nodded. With two fingers, he pulled out one side of the fox's muzzle to make a little pouch leading down to the throat. He took the pitcher from Retta with his free hand.

At the first few drops of liquid, the fox struggled inside the towel wrappings, then lay still except for the quick red tongue lapping at the medicine. Dallas talked to the animal as he poured the droplets slowly, patiently, soothing it with the sound of his voice.

In moments, the brandy and the aspirin took effect and the fox was as languid as a sleeping child. Dobson placed it gently in the wicker basket, still in its toweling wrap, and then covered the top with the other big towel, tucking the edges in tight.

"That should do it," he said, and touched Retta's hand in the darkness. "We should know by morning."

"It's so late," she said. "Let me make you a bed on the couch in the library."

"No," he said firmly. "I'll lie right here. It wouldn't be right to sleep in your house unless your parents asked me to."

"But they're not like that," she protested. "I told you that before. . . ."

"See you in the morning," he said.

She did not hurry. She waited until she had brushed

her hair and teeth and slipped into a long-sleeved nightgown before she went into the hallway to turn off the upstairs light. She touched the switch and waited until her eyes were accustomed to the darkness outside.

The night was moonless, lit only by the far light of stars, yet as she looked down she felt she could see him clearly, a lanky figure curved in a half circle around the fox's basket, covered by a towel. There was something private, almost intimate, in that moment. She shivered, though from something other than cold. *I know so much about him now,* she thought. *So much more than just what he tried to tell me.*

Chapter
7

It was not the dawn sunlight that waked her, but the awareness that someone was in her room. She opened her eyes to see her father sitting on the edge of the bed in blue jeans and shirt, with the sleeves of an old cashmere sweater knotted around his neck. A mug of coffee steamed on the night table.

"Poppy, why are you awake so early?"

"I didn't really wake up, Princess. I just didn't seem to get to sleep last night."

"But I knocked and — " She sat up suddenly, with the memory of Dallas and the sick fox. Her eyes turned to the bedroom window overlooking the back lawn.

"He's gone," her father said. "I drove him over to

the vet's about an hour ago. Doc Stewart was on night duty. Then I dropped him at the Kennellys'."

"You saw him? You've met him?"

Her father nodded. "I did. And I just wanted to have a few words with you before the family wakes up."

Retta felt the dryness of panic in her throat. "And the fox? What about our fox?"

"That young vixen has a strep throat," her father said. "Sick as a skunk, or a fox in this case. The vet has her caged. He's going to keep her on antibiotics for a little while. He believes the fox would have died out there if you hadn't found her."

"Last night I tried to get your advice."

"Don't worry," he said. "Young Dobson told me what you did. Warmth, aspirin, food, and a little stimulant. You did the right thing."

Through the dim morning light, Henrietta realized her father's face was grave, subdued, and he seemed to be watching her closely. "Nice lad," he said, "but he was lucky he didn't get bitten. Wild foxes often have rabies, you know."

"He was careful. And, as I said, I tried to ask you what to do."

He took a sip of the hot coffee, then handed the mug to his daughter. "I know you did, Retta. And I should have come out to talk with you, but, well. . . ." He paused and looked at her thoughtfully, somewhat embarrassed, almost too young for the faint wrinkles in the forehead, the touches of gray in his hair. "It was an important night. I'm going to fly out to California today on business. And sometimes it's hard saying good-bye, if only for a day or two. I hope you understand that, Retta."

A rush of deep emotion and affection swept through her as she understood his words.

She sipped the coffee until she felt sure her voice was under control. "Of course, Poppy," she said. "Of course."

"I'm afraid, Retta, that with all the worry about business at the paper and about that damned highway, your mother and I haven't been giving you the time and attention we ought to. I know you're growing up, but I don't want you to grow away from us. Not yet, anyway."

He paused and his next question, though light and casual in tone, brought a quick touch of color to his daughter's cheeks. "How long have you been seeing young Dobson?" he asked.

"I don't really *see* him, not in the way you mean," she said. "We don't date or anything. I just drive him to school each day."

"*Every* day?"

"Yes, when he can make it. He hitchhikes to the Kennellys' where he's a stable boy. I take him from there. They have a pickup truck, but his father needs it to get to work."

"But you were with him last night."

"Yes, I was. We were studying together at Charlotte's. You see, he had to drop out of school for two years and he's way behind. He came to Havendale High to try to catch up."

"He's new in these parts?"

She nodded vigorously. "Yes, he and his father

just moved back here from Texas. His father is Daniel Dobson; he works at the feed store."

"Danny Dobson?"

"Well, I guess so. You mean you know him?"

"Not really. He was a friend of a friend, before he left Zenith." He paused, frowning a little, as if trying to sort out his thoughts. "But isn't Dobson a little old for you? The Danny Dobson I knew had a son. He'd be about twenty-five by now."

"That would be his brother Sam Houston. He was killed in an accident more than three years ago. Dallas is eighteen, going on nineteen. About two years older than I. Maybe he seemed older to you because he's so tall."

"What concerns me, Retta, is that you've driven this young man to school many times, even dozens of times, and yet you never mentioned him to me or your mother."

Retta felt a sting of tears in her eyes as she heard the rebuke in her father's voice. "There is nothing to tell, really," she said. "Absolutely nothing. We go to the same school. We're good friends, that's all."

"About that fox," her father said obliquely. "Doc Stewart says you can pick it up in about three days. Take it back to the spot you found it, and let it loose. If its lair is nearby, it can backtrack home."

He rose and walked to the door. "If I'm still in California, maybe young Dobson can help you. I'm taking you at your word, Henrietta. Just good friends."

He had already stepped into the hallway when she made up her mind and called after him. "Wait

72

a minute, Poppy. I almost forgot to give something to you."

She put her feet on the cold floor without bothering with slippers and went to her closet. Inside, hanging on a hook, was her red school purse. She unzipped the inner compartment and took out something which she handed to her father.

"I know you're executor of Aunt Blue's estate. This is for her house. It's an extra key."

As it turned out, Carter Caldwell was delayed in California, Dallas Dobson was absent from school three days in a row, and Retta had to return the fox to the woods herself. Dr. Stewart had put the animal in a wire cat-carrier. It was completely healed, transformed again into a feisty, wild creature, alert and unafraid, its thick, bushy tail sweeping nervously back and forth, eyes bright and sly as Retta carried the cage to the car.

The weather had turned cold and this morning a deep, penetrating chill froze the muddy backroads into iron ruts and caught the fox's breath in a frosty white cloud just off the end of its nose.

Retta parked her car where it had been parked four nights before and took the cat-cage from the car. The road was deserted. She set the cage on the ground, then blew on her cold fingers to limber them before unsnapping the double-wire door. The fox seemed to hesitate a moment, the tip of its black leather nose inched just a wary step toward freedom. Then it darted toward the woods, leaping the roadside ditch in a single graceful arc that knocked dew-frost from the bushes.

There was the sharp sound of boots on the frozen ground, and Retta turned to see Dobson running toward her from the Kennelly farm, books under his arm, one hand raised in a wave.

"I wanted to be with you," he shouted and then, as he came closer, "I just couldn't help it, Retta. I've been working days at the feed store for my father. He drinks, you know. Not always, but more lately."

"Let's get in the car," she said. "I should have worn gloves."

She turned on the car heater and a waft of warm air touched their faces, smelling, after six months' disuse, of dust, oil, and the sticky scent of rubber. Dallas put his books on the floor and sank low in his seat, his long legs tucked under the dashboard. He tried to warm his hands by rubbing them on the denim of his sharp knees. Retta noticed at once his broken fingernails, and the deep burn, red and crusted, along the back of one hand.

He put his healthy hand over the burn defensively. "I told you I didn't want you to be sorry for me," he said. "I'm just trying to decide what it is I'm responsible for, what my father expects of me, and what I owe him." He paused.

"He drinks when he's blue or angry, and then I can't reason with him. Last night he began shouting that he missed Sam Houston more than any man could be expected to stand. He said he didn't want Sam's things around anymore to remind him that Sam Houston was dead. He said he never wanted me to mention my brother's name again. He shouted those things over and over, like he was trying to convince himself they would work some kind of magic with his feelings. That they'd help him to forget somehow.

"Then he tried to burn Sam's clothes, even his music, and when I pulled the stuff out of the fireplace, well — I got burned, that's all." He rubbed a hand over his forehead savagely, as if to brush away thoughts he didn't want to be there.

"He's sick, I know that, because he's got terrible angers inside his head and he's afraid to face them or try to get rid of them. I have to feel sorry for the man. I know he hurts in his leg and in his heart and his head and everywhere else, for that matter. But I don't seem to know how to help him, that's what's so hard on me. And I think he ought to realize how much I miss Sam Houston, too."

A light snow flurry had begun and soft flakes stuck to the windshield. Retta turned on the wipers, welcoming the sound and rhythmic movement in the tense silence of the car.

"I shouldn't dump on you, Retta," he said, "but I'm not finding any answers. Last night I put my hand in the fire for my brother because I don't want to forget him, or lose things he had touched. It *can't* be right to pretend that that great guy just never *was*. But my father. . . ." He paused and sighed. "I wish my father was like that fox back there — a healthy animal with nothing but a sore throat, something so simple I could make him well and set him free. . . ."

Chapter
8

The state of Pennsylvania sits in a hybrid location, about four states south of chilly Canada, yet above the Mason-Dixon line and the warmer climate of the South. Sometimes the weather stays moderate, spongy ground and soft wind so full of warmth and moisture that yellow forsythia can be duped into blooming at Christmas time. In another year, snows and winds can drift over the fields and highway long before Thanksgiving. Blizzards in that state can blow up as quickly as a squall over water.

This year the first storm came the fourth Tuesday in November, a few drifting flakes in the early morning, with a stiff wind and a thick mist of granular snow by ten o'clock. At Havendale High, the storm coated the north side of trees and blanketed school buses and parked cars, a shifting, drifting cover of white that glistened with sharp, frozen crystals.

By lunch hour, the storm was blowing in full fury, singing winds sounding at every window and driving snow adding to the soft, flaky ground cover in a slick, dangerous layer. The sky was dark and a leaden gray, as devoid of sunlight as if someone had pulled an off-switch. A county snowplow pushed into the school parking lot, backing and filing, until its great metal blade cleared driving paths from the school to the main road.

At the end of the three-o'clock class, the principal's voice sounded over the loudspeaker system. "We're canceling all further classes for the day," he said. "The county highway department has issued a bulletin that we're in for a real blow. All students depending on school buses for transportation go directly to the west parking lot. All students providing self-transportation are advised to go straight home. I repeat: Students with self-transportation are advised to go straight home."

Retta cupped her hand over her mouth and nose to keep out the knife-sharp cold as she ran for her parked car. Already the cars looked alike, humped and white with snow, but she recognized the Volkswagen at once. Dallas Dobson was standing beside it, hands in his pockets, stomping his feet sharply on the hard-packed snow.

"One more favor, Retta," he said quickly. "I need a lift to the Kennellys'. I tried to call but the lines must be down. I've got to spend the night there.

Those Arabians are on a feeding schedule, six tonight and six in the morning. They'd get colic or kick their stalls into splinters if they missed a meal. The old man could get out to the barns tonight, maybe, but with this storm, I know he can't make it in the morning."

"Quick then," she said. The windshield wipers cleared little arcs of vision on the snow-crusted glass. Retta put the car in reverse and caught her breath as the rear wheels spun without traction on the slick snow. She tried again with greater speed, and in moments the car was turned toward the exit gate, following a school bus that was tailgating Junior Provanza's red Porsche, roofed and dappled now with hard snow.

The plow-cleared main highway was easy, but turning into the tertiary road that led to the Kennellys' was like entering a different world, ominous and silent. No one had traveled this lane in several hours and the snow was unmarked by tires. Eddies of snow swirled over the surface and it was difficult to know where the sides of the road ended and the ditches began.

Retta proceeded with caution, holding the steering wheel firmly, hoping to feel the security of tires cutting through the snow and down to the hard, graveled surface. But the car seemed to wallow and shift in the deepening drifts.

A half mile in, Dallas peered through the windshield and said, "Let me off here, Retta. I'll walk in and you go back."

He touched her cheek lightly with his cold fingers and got out of the car. But the smooth surface of the snow was deceiving. He sank deep over his boot tops and went floundering forward, buffeted by the wind and struggling like a man in deep water.

She turned down her window a crack and shouted into the wind. "Dallas, you'll never make it. We'll have to get back to the main road and wait for the snowplows. I'll try backing out."

She put the car in reverse and looked through the rear window, but could see nothing through the falling snow. The wheels spun, kicking up snow and bits of gravel, but the car settled into a rut and would not move. She gunned the motor but heard Dobson shout, "No more! You're just digging yourself in!"

He worked in silence for a few minutes and she saw what he intended to do. With his gloveless hands, he tore at the snow-wet wineberry bushes and gathered up armloads of weathered goldenrod, pulling the brittle plants up by the roots. He laid the bundled material behind the rear wheels and then plodded up to the driver's side of the car. "Move over," he said. "Let me try."

Slowly, carefully, he tried to urge the car backward, hoping the tires would find traction on the bushes and branches. The wheels spun, gripped, then spun again. "We need one more booster," he said, and went back into the snow. The field at the side of the road was fenced with a split-rail barrier, long weathered timbers of locust trees laid one on top of the other in a tongue-and-groove structure.

With a powerful wrench, Dallas loosened the top rail and carried it back to the road, jamming it tightly under the two rear wheels.

This time the tires caught on the solid wood and began to inch backward. "All right, Retta," he said quietly. "I'm going to try to follow our tire tracks back to the main road." He switched on the headlights and the beams shot yellow shafts through the whorls of snow. "We don't want to hit anyone coming *or* going," he said. "You be my eyes out front, and I'll try to watch the back."

Leaning hard on the horn, he began to inch the car backwards. The shrill, insistent sound of the horn seemed to be picked up by the wind and echo around them in all directions. The minutes seemed like hours, and the winding lane an endless blur of drifts and danger. At last the main road showed in the rearview mirror, and the rear wheels of the car hit solid macadam.

There were no other cars in sight and the broad, cleared strokes made by the snowplow had already begun to catch shifting drifts of snow. "We can worry about the horses later," Dallas Dobson said. "I'm getting you home."

From the first moment inside her own house, Retta sensed that something wasn't right, but she could not say what it was.

Her mother met them as they came in the front door, stamping the snow off their feet on the mat. With extended hand, she said, "You must be Dallas Dobson," even before Retta could speak. Their Irish setter, Gypsy, sniffed the young man's boots and wagged her feathered tail. "See, the dog likes you already. Come in, come in." Mrs. Caldwell smiled again. "And now that you're here, you must spend the night. I insist on it. We're all just country folks in weather like this."

When Dobson looked doubtful, she put a hand on his arm. "My husband phoned to say he's sleeping at the office because Highway 111 is completely blocked. You just phone home and tell whomever is there that you're staying with the Caldwells."

"No one at home is going to worry about me," he said, "but I had planned to hike back to the Kennellys'. I can't reach them by phone. Mr. Kennelly can get out for tonight's feed, but I've got to be there tomorrow. I take care of their Arabians, you see."

"Don't you worry, young man," Mrs. Caldwell said. "If the storm is so bad that we can't get my car out by daybreak, I'll lend you my husband's cross-country skis."

When Dallas Dobson suggested he try to dig out the walks and snowbanks that were drifting around the closed doors of the garage, Mrs. Caldwell's answer was strangely personal and condescending. "Don't feel you have to work for your supper. You're perfectly welcome in this house, Dallas."

Dobson said simply, "We get snow in Texas sometimes. It's best to dig out before it gets the best of you."

Retta stayed in her room most of the late afternoon. Her mother had turned on a rock station on the kitchen radio and the steady beat filtered up through the old house, making it difficult to concentrate. Retta sat on the window seat and played Spanish language tapes on her cassette deck. It pleased her to drown out the music from the kitchen with the precise, accented voice of someone outside the family. From the window, she could see Dobson clearing the walks, working rapidly, rhythmically, throwing shovels of snow in great arcs on either side of the paths. He had taken off his windbreaker and hung it on the branch of a small apple tree. Even in the cold, his denim shirt clung to him, and Retta could see the dark stain of perspiration between his shoulder blades. From somewhere inside the house, someone turned on the yard lights.

There was a tap on her door and Two said, "Mother asks you to go tell your boyfriend that dinner is ready. He can wash up in my room. He's going to sleep there, too."

The kitchen was empty when Retta went downstairs, but she noticed at once the elaborate preparations for dinner; a chicken and cashew nut casserole from her mother's "emergency shelf" in the freezer had been heated in the oven. There was a tossed green salad and a silver basket of fresh cornmeal muffins, as small as pigeon eggs.

Retta pushed open the door to the dining room and gave an involuntary gasp of surprise. The table had been set with their best Lenox china and crystal. On the sideboard stood a tray with fluted glasses of raspberries and small cups for after-dinner coffee. In the center of the table was a china pot of flowering begonias. Tall, pink tapers burned brightly in Grand-mama Caldwell's silver candlesticks. Retta tried to stifle a feeling of confusion and concern, emotions so intense that her cheeks felt aflame.

Her thoughts were churning. *What was the fuss all about?* she wondered. *Would Dallas, just a Texas cowhand, really — he told you that right away — would he feel awkward and out of place with all that silver and candlelight?* There seemed no direct clue, no guidelines to what was happening. Her mother was always a good hostess. It was like Mrs. Caldwell to prepare an interesting dinner for a guest, but this was too much like a party, too much like showing off. What *was* it all about? It couldn't all be just for Dallas and the three Caldwells, Retta thought. It was like her mother was play-acting, trying to impress someone else, almost as if another guest were expected to join them at dinner. *Why?*

In the kitchen, Retta snapped off the blaring radio, then called to Dallas from the back door, grateful for cold wind on her face. He removed his jacket from the apple tree, then carefully tamped snow off the shovel before propping it near the back door. Someone, Retta saw, had already located her father's cross-country skis and leaned them against the door.

But there was no chance to run upstairs and ask her mother questions in private. And since she didn't quite understand her own roiling emotions, her almost violently protective feelings toward Dallas and his pride, Retta couldn't decide just what those questions ought to be.

Mrs. Caldwell came through the swinging door of the kitchen wearing a long plaid hostess skirt and a low-necked red sweater. Small pearl earrings matched a double string of pearls, and with every movement she wafted the odor of spicy cologne.

"Ah, you two," she said lightly. "Five minutes till dinner. Retta, perhaps you'd like to freshen up, and you can show your friend to Two's quarters. He'll be bunking there tonight."

When she got to her own room, Two, standing at the bathroom sink, called through the half-open door. "Your boyfriend is gonna use my space. I'll be through here right away."

A few moments later, he stepped out for inspection, his face shining, blond hair plastered down with water. "Do I look okay?"

"You look as good as you can," she said sharply, not trying to mask her emotion and anger. "Why is she *doing* this to me, Two? To me *and* to Dallas?"

"Doing what?"

"You know as well as I do. Best china, raspberries . . . even candles."

"We always have candles in the dining room," he said. "You know that."

"But we don't always *light* them," she said, "as you darn well know."

"I don't know what you're mad at *me* for," Two said, hurt and defensive.

"It's just by *chance* that he's here at all. It's freaky weather. He didn't *plan* it this way. Why can't she just be natural? Can't she realize he's just a boy, an ordinary person?"

84

"Gee, Retta," he said. "Keep your voice down. Why don't you just come out and say you love the guy?"

She stared at her brother in disbelief and when she spoke her tone was low, almost savage. "Why, you irresponsible little freak! Get out of here this minute! And don't ever come into my room again without permission. Not *ever*!"

When he left, she stood at the bathroom sink splashing cold water on her face until she could no longer feel the tears, hot and unwanted on her cheeks. *Why did I do that?* she thought sadly. *Two, of all people. But why did he say that about love? What is happening to me?*

When she at last went downstairs, the others were already seated at the candle-lit table, and there was a plate of chicken casserole at her place.

Dallas rose as Retta entered the room, and moved to pull out her chair. She seated herself and he pushed the chair back into place, lightly touching the back of her neck with his fingers, still stiff and chilled from the snow. When he seated himself again, Retta looked across the table at him and saw him smile, not a laughing, open smile, but just a quick movement of the lips and a flash of warmth in the eyes. For a moment she felt tears again in her own eyes.

He knows I've been crying, she thought. *He knows but he doesn't know why; yet, whatever it is, he wants to make it right. Of course he's a Texas cowhand, but he's my Texas cowhand. He's thinking about me. He doesn't care about the candles and the silver and the little fluted glasses on the side-board. Dallas Dobson cares about how I feel, he cares about me.*

Connie Caldwell passed her daughter the silver basket of muffins, but Retta shook her head, then forced herself to concentrate on the bright, flickering flame of the candles, demanding her emotions to subside, her cheeks to cool. Splintered thoughts ran through her mind like quicksilver: He touched me, he smiled. There is a table between us, there are other people here, but he and I are completely together in this room. . . .

Her thoughts were so intense, so singing with conviction in her brain, that she did not hear her mother speak. Connie Caldwell had asked, "Not hungry, Retta? You're not eating a thing."

Chapter
9

The sun was muted in a clouded gray sky, and Retta had to check her bedside clock to see if morning had come. It was a few minutes after seven. She had overslept.

She hurried to the window overlooking the front drive to see if he had left, but the roadway was drifted over, as smooth as frozen cream. She saw a crisscross of wild bird tracks and the light, patterned trail of a woods rabbit, but no mark of tires or skis.

She reached for her robe. I must wake him, she thought. He must get to the horses. A moment like this had never happened before and she was almost weak with anticipation and excitement. *I can touch his shoulder,* she thought. *I can watch him open his eyes.*

But the extra bed in Two's room was empty and made up, a blue blanket neatly folded at the foot. Her brother was still asleep, arms curled under his head. Stepping softly, Retta went to a window and pulled up the shade on a dormer overlooking the rear of the house and the sloping meadow. The answer was there. He was gone. A pair of ski tracks traced a curving path over the crusted snow, disappearing off beyond the big farm pond.

How clever, she thought, with a touch of sadness. He's taking a shortcut to the Kennellys'. How country-smart, how ingenious to know the right thing to do. But she suddenly felt lonely and small and left out. He had done what he had to do. He hadn't needed her help after all.

A light wind sprang up, sending little whorls of white across the ground. Even as she watched, her forehead pressed against the cold windowpane, Retta saw snow blow into the narrow ski ruts, almost wiping from sight any trace of his passage.

By Monday all the main roads had been plowed open, but Dallas Dobson was not at school. On Tuesday, his desk was empty again. On the third morning, he hurried in just as the last bell rang. When Mr. Engel stood at the blackboard, diagramming a problem, Dallas passed her a scrawled note which read: *Sorry, sorry. Snowed in with the horses. Provanza is my transport. He's got his father's four-wheeler and chains.*

She nodded her head and felt the sudden warmth as he leaned forward and touched his fingers to the back of her neck.

Mr. Engel asked to see Dobson after class and, though she waited for him outside the classroom, he did not come and she had to hurry to make Señora Escudero's class.

By noontime a winter sun broke through the gray clouds. Pale light glittered off the massive drifts left by snowplows, and sent rivulets of water streaming across the parking lot. The snowman someone had built on the school's west lawn turned soft and wet. First it lost its black coal eyes and then its broom.

Alone in her room that evening, Retta took the note from the pages of her math book and smoothed it out under the light of a reading lamp. There were only a dozen or so words on the paper and they told her no more at that moment than they had in the classroom this morning. But she read the note again and again, then shut her eyes and ran her fingers over and over the thick, blunt handwriting, as if she were trying to extract new meaning from the words through a kind of emotional braille.

Sometime during the night, the hall phone rang and waked Retta from troubled dreams. She heard her father, who had come home, answer, say a few quick words, and then the house was quiet again, but she could not go back to sleep. With a blanket around her shoulders, she sat in the curve of the window seat, staring out into the darkness. The night was filled with liquid noises as snow melted into the roof gutters, and icicles on the eaves shortened by every drip. The big fir trees had dropped their load of wet snow and now stood black and stark along the drive. It was going. As quickly as the storm had come, it began to melt away.

During lunch hour, the principal's voice came over the loudspeaker system to remind the student body that there would be a countywide teachers' meeting in West Chester that afternoon, and all students were requested to be off campus by two o'clock.

Even before she went out to her yellow car, Retta knew that Dallas would be waiting for her. "We both have time today," he said simply. "I'd like you to see how *I* live. *We* live, I should say."

"Do you want to drive?" she asked, and he nodded.

The car followed the main road for about three miles and then Dobson turned toward backcountry, passing Provanza's market, and then down onto a gravel and dirt road that traveled away from the fenced and well-groomed farms and estates and through a grubby settlement with sleeper vans, rusting mobile homes, and a few rundown clapboard houses in an area called Little Tennessee. Here clothes fluttered from a wire line behind every residence, and in front of most there was a thin, fierce watchdog, tugging and barking at the end of a short chain.

Beyond Little Tennessee were a few makeshift country places with chickens in the front yard and relics of broken-down cars and farm machinery in the back. Here the flat fields were stubbled with rotting pumpkins and snow-wet cornstalks, and even the grazing land was poor, rough with stones and hummocks and scattered with cow dung.

Finally, Dallas made a sharp right and smiled at her without joy. "We're over on Snuff Mill Road," he said. In this area, Zenith River ran fast, full now from melting snows, still turning the old waterwheel at the snuff mill, a red-brick shambles of a building a century old, perched at the edge of the stream. Beyond the mill was a long, single street with narrow, brick houses on both sides. Most of the structures were in ruin but eight had been brought back to use, windowpanes in place, roofs and front porches in good repair.

Dallas pulled up in front of the last house. A rough drive curved round to a backyard shed. The house and the street seemed to be deserted. There were no children at play, no wandering pets, no movement or sound anywhere except the creak of the waterwheel and the frothing rush of the old mill stream.

Dallas unlocked the front door and held it open for Retta. Inside, he took her short red coat and hung it on a coatrack made of moose antlers. "Here's where I live," he said, gesturing with a sweep of his hand.

It was a small room with a rag rug in the middle of the floor, some rodeo posters tacked to the walls, a table and chairs, and one long, worn couch in cracked, brown leather. There were andirons in the fireplace but no sign of logs or kindling, not even a sprinkling of ashes. It had been swept clean. The windows, without curtains, had green shades pulled so low now that the room was almost dark.

"The kitchen is behind that door. Upstairs there are two bedrooms and a bath," Dallas Dobson said. "One room's a kind of storage space, and my father sleeps in the other one."

He pointed to the corner table and then the couch. "I study over there and I sleep here," he said. "I cook and I keep things clean."

The couch sagged with years and wear, a nest of worn leather and broken springs, with a plaid horse-blanket folded neatly at one end. And there was one fancy lavender pillow with an embroidered cover of pansies trimmed in lace.

Retta could feel Dallas looking at her, searching her face, gauging her reactions to what she saw. She had a strong urge to stand close to him, touch his young, serious face, and whisper, "Please believe me. It's all right. It doesn't matter. . . ."

Instead, she managed to say, "It's very nice."

He shrugged and moved toward her and his voice was close and husky. "I've lived in worse places," he said.

Suddenly, from overhead, there was a heavy but muted movement, the creak of bed springs, the sound of boots on the floor. Dallas winced visibly and clenched his hands. They stood as they were, close together, and neither spoke as they heard the sound of rubber-tipped crutches moving across the bedroom, over to the top of the stairs. Slowly, moving as if each step were painful, they saw first the crutches, then the cowboy boots of Danny Dobson as he moved cautiously down the flight of uncarpeted stairs.

Retta stared as if mesmerized until the man was standing directly in front of her, his weight balanced heavily on the padded crutches supporting him under each arm.

Retta felt she had never seen a better-looking man, lean and broad-shouldered, with thick, fair hair and eyes that were blue and steady as azure marbles. Danny Dobson stared at her almost impersonally, letting his gaze check out her face, her unsteady smile, and then the contours of her body. He was frankly appraising and sardonic in his judgment of the young woman standing before him.

He swayed a little on the crutches, then shivered as if his knees gave him pain. When he smiled at her, Retta caught the sharp, rancid smell of liquor and realized the man had been drinking, but his voice was cold and scathing as he spoke. "I guess you two didn't figure I'd be home this time of day, right?"

Dallas shrugged and said simply, "It's your home as well as mine," and then, "This is Henrietta Caldwell. Retta, my father, Daniel Dobson."

Dobson moved forward a step on his crutches and held out his hand. Retta took it and found it hard and smooth and surprisingly cool, not matching the anger in the man's eyes.

"Caldwell," he said, still holding her hand. "You look it. The same airs. A Caldwell through and through. . . . Just what I might have expected."

"That's it, Father," Dallas said sharply. "You've said enough."

Daniel Dobson dropped the girl's hand and wheeled around sharply on his crutches, putting one hand on the mantelpiece for support, staring down at the cold, empty fireplace, his shoulders heaved with emotion, almost a dry sobbing, as he struggled to bring himself under control.

Then he turned and spoke to his son. "They drove me home early because my legs hurt and because I got a little drunk on the job. Maybe you can pick up the truck down at the feed store." He tried to smile at them both but his eyes were opaque and without warmth. He punched his son lightly on the arm. "Come on. Don't be tough on the old man, kid. You know how I get sometimes. . . ."

Outside, Dallas rolled down the car window on the driver's side and drove the next five miles at top speed, without speaking, to the feed store where his father worked. A battered pickup truck was parked at one side of a weighing shed.

When he got out of the car, Retta slid behind the wheel and set the shift for reverse, but Dallas leaned on the open window, as if willing her to stay. He stared at her thoughtfully for several moments. His eyes were not steel-blue like his father's, but a deep gray-green with flecks of brown, and his young face was infinitely sad as he reached in to put his big hand on Retta's as it rested on the steering wheel. He held it so tightly that her bones hurt and she could feel the pulse of blood in the veins, so full and steady that she did not know if it came from his heartbeat or her own.

"No matter what you think, Retta," he said at last, "I still love him. And he's part of whatever I am."

"I know that," she said. "You don't have to tell me. But. . . ." She paused. "I think you're also afraid of him."

"No, no," he said with sharp conviction. "It's the other way around. He's afraid of *me*. He's crippled, he doesn't have Sam Houston anymore. And he's afraid I might leave him some day."

"And you never will?" she asked.

"I don't know," he said. He took his hand from hers and jammed it deep in his jeans pocket. "That's something I can't tell you."

On the Friday after Thanksgiving, Mr. Engel opened his classroom and gave Dallas Dobson a private test. Dobson passed junior geometry with a B-plus, and was immediately assigned to a senior group studying basic trigonometry.

Retta still drove him to school most mornings, but the daily meetings in math class and the study sessions at the Ambersons' were over.

Chapter
10

Carter Caldwell made two more trips to California, one in the last week of December. He promised his family he would be home for Christmas, and Retta thought it was her father's car early on Christmas Eve as a pair of headlights turned in the drive and slashed through the darkness. But it was Dallas Dobson in a pickup truck.

He knocked at the back door, carrying a Jerusalem cherry plant, the dark leaves glossy as green leather, the plump, round fruit a bright red-orange. It had begun to snow and when Retta opened the door and stepped outside, she saw a few feathery flakes had settled on his hair and made a white fringe of his eyelashes. *How lovely and how sad,* she thought. *I now know how he will look as a very old man.*

"What a nice gift, Dallas," she was able to say warmly. Then, "But I'm embarrassed. I have nothing for you. I didn't know we were going to do this."

"I just wanted something for *you*," he said as she took the plant. "It isn't much, I know."

"It's *everything*," she said impetuously. "We'll use it for a centerpiece tomorrow. And you *will* come for Christmas dinner. I know my parents will say yes."

"I can't do that," he said. "I'm cooking at my house. My father won the turkey raffle at the feed store and I'm fixing it. He's invited some lady he knows."

"You can cook a turkey?" she said with surprise.

He nodded. "A turkey, the dressing, some sweet potatoes, and cranberries. I bought those canned." Retta found herself smiling, almost without meaning to. "And I've just about decided I'm going to try to make pumpkin pie."

She knew her smile might turn to laughter, so she held the Christmas plant in one arm and embraced him with the other. She held him tight, her face pressed against the smooth, cold fabric of his windbreaker, laughter almost smothered. "I'm not laughing *at* you," she said in a choking voice. "I'm laughing *with* you. A pumpkin pie. . . ."

He was silent, not moving, and she looked up quickly, afraid she might have hurt his feelings. But he was smiling at her, and kissed her mouth until the laughter died away.

A few moments later, she brought the Christmas plant into the dining room. Her mother turned from setting the table and said, "What was so funny out there, Retta? I heard all that noise."

"There's no way to explain, Mother," she said. "Dallas Dobson just said he could bake a pumpkin pie."

It had long been a tradition at Havendale High School, since it was founded more than eight decades ago, to hold the senior prom early in the second semester. In the old days, male students from working farm families were released from school on May first so they could help with the plowing and planting and get the meadows ready for summer pasturing. So the prom was always held in the school gym on the first Friday night after Valentine's Day.

"It's the fifteenth," Dallas said to her one morning on the way to school. "I've got enough credits now to qualify as a senior. I'd like you to go with me. We can double-date with Junior Provanza and Charlotte Amberson. He told me he's going to ask her."

Retta decided on silence about Charlotte. Just last evening, late, when Mrs. Amberson was sleeping, Charlie had called her to tell her that Junior Provanza had called about the prom and her mother insisted she turn him down. "It's not just Junior," Charlie had said. "And not just because he's a butcher, but that doesn't help either. My mother will never think *anyone* is good enough for me."

"I've wanted to ask you out other times," Dobson continued, "but I just can't. I've been saving money, you see. One of the times when I thought my father was off drinking somewhere, well, he told me that he'd really gone into Philadelphia that day to see a bone specialist. His legs *can* be fixed, Retta. He told me that. But the operation is expensive. He has no insurance and the feed store won't help out because the accident happened before he came to work for them." He put his hand slightly on her shoulder, then tightened his grip until she winced. "Think what it could mean," he said, "for a man like that to *walk* without crutches again." He paused. "My father doesn't know it, but I've been saving money for that operation."

"We could go halves on expenses for the dance," she said. "I get paid, you know, for delivering that society column each morning."

"No," he said quickly. "I'm only going to have one prom in my lifetime, and I want the whole thing. I want to buy the tickets, I want you to tell me what color you're wearing, and let me pick the corsage. I want to pick you up at your house for once. I want to do everything I'm supposed to do."

"Then I'll tell you about my dress later," she said. "I'll try to find something in Zenith."

"I know you have almost a month," her mother said later that afternoon, "but why not drive with us to Philadelphia on Saturday? Carter feels we're getting nowhere with the people in Harrisburg. He wants to consult with an experienced lawyer, Luis Berger, in Philadelphia. Someone who's an expert on the 'Right of Eminent Domain.' We'll drop you at Bonwit's and pick you up after our appointment."

Retta spent two hours at the big store, examining the collection of formal wear, and she tried on a dozen before narrowing her choice down to two: a full-length, strapless dress of soft red organza; and a full-skirted gown with cap sleeves and a rounded neckline, the whole thing made up of rows and rows of pale blue and green lace.

When she put on the red dress for the second time, the saleslady had said, "We'll have the seamstress loosen it a little under the arms. You're quite busty, young lady. Otherwise, it's perfect."

When her parents arrived in front of Bonwit's to pick her up, Retta asked her father if he could drive around the block a few times while her mother helped her to decide.

The saleslady held out both dresses on hangers, moving them a little to show their lines and flow. Mrs. Caldwell cocked her head and was silent for some time. Then she said, "It really all depends on you, Retta. What is your aura these days? Would you say you're more blue-green? Or are you in a red phase of your personality?"

Retta felt a spasm of frustration. "Mother," she said impatiently. "Mother, I wanted your advice, not some pop psychology. I'm all mixed up. How do I know what my *aura* is? Don't say anything more. Let me do it by myself."

Retta closed her eyes and turned around three times, then reached out toward the two party dresses. As her fingers closed on the light, soft fabric, she knew she would be wearing red.

* * *

The senior decorating committee had been sworn
to secrecy, so the transformation of the gym was a
surprise. It was decorated as a surrealist nightclub
with black and white streamers, dozens of clusters
of matching balloons, and chairs with small tables,
alternately clothed in black and white. The lights
were covered with silver cellophane so the whole
room had a misty, moonlit quality.

Dallas had picked two white gardenias on a red
ribbon as a corsage, and Retta tied them on her
wrist. For himself, he had rented a deep blue tuxedo
with a white ruffled shirt, and with his hair long to
the collar, his manner grave and subdued, Retta
thought he looked like some handsome courtier out
of the Middle Ages. He was much taller than she
(and wearing those old, shined-up Texas boots with
stacked heels) and when they danced, he held her
close, her face almost buried in the froth of white
ruffles. He was a confident dancer only to slow
music, but she did not mind sitting out every other
set.

Halfway through the evening, Junior Provanza came
into the gym, guiding his twin sister, Parma, his date
for the evening. Parma often liked to tell school
friends that her mother had explained to her that
she had been born first, the dominant twin, and that
was why she was bulkier and at least a head taller
than her brother. Her prom dress was of deep blue
velvet, off-the-shoulder, and Parma had selected el-
bow-length white kid gloves to wear with it. Her
dark hair was groomed into a thick, bell-like page

101

boy that curled just under the chin line. Like most of the girls, her eye makeup was heavy, and deep red lipstick set off the unhappy pout of her lips.

"Momma says I gotta go with Junior," she had explained to Henrietta a few days earlier. "The guy I like is in the Army, and Junior's got some love problem. He won't talk about it, but he's just *sick* over someone.

"I'm gonna borrow an outfit from my cousin, kind of early-Grace-Kelly stuff. It just doesn't seem right to buy a formal just to dance with your brother."

The two Provanzas stood together at the edge of the dance floor, both sullen and self-conscious, till Retta whispered to Dallas, "Let's dance over and switch partners a few times. I mean, it's the senior prom for them, too."

Dallas and Retta exchanged dances with the twins three times before several other couples sensed what was going on and asked the Provanzas to exchange dances also.

The decorating committee had covered the big gym clock with black and white streamers, so time seemed to float by, unmarked, with no way to check the hours. Between dances, Dallas managed to hold Retta's hand, lightly, warmly, and he kept his fingers on her wrist, a small, intimate gesture, even when Mr. Engel and his wife had joined them at a black and white table.

Without watching the hands or hearing the tick of a clock, Retta was aware of the swift passage of time, the excitement, the fresh wonder that brushed over the whole evening for her. Dancing, sitting at the tables, she felt calm and poised, yet moved with an almost giddy happiness.

What if I kept a diary? she thought to herself as she and Dallas moved through a smooth, almost liquid, dance number, his shirtfront soft and clean as clover against her cheek. *What would I write in it about tonight? I don't know, I just don't know for sure,* an inner voice whispered back to her. *I think I would leave the pages blank. I would put down nothing at all, just leave the pages untouched for years and years until I could remember everything with clarity and depth, and then search my mind for the right words, the forever-words to put my feelings on paper. I am still Henrietta Caldwell, but tonight I just want to feel, not think or speak. Or ask myself any questions.*

To signal the last dance, to let the prom crowd know the evening was almost over, Mr. Engel stood at the control panel and turned the decorated gym lights down low, low, and lower until the big room was dimmed into an artificial twilight.

As they moved together to the music, Dallas bent down to whisper, "Henrietta, is it like what you wanted it to be?"

She squeezed his hand in an affirmative answer, and he tightened his arm on her shoulders, moved and exhilarated by her gentle, wordless "Yes."

Yet, as he drove her home, Dallas fell silent. He steered with one hand on the wheel, the other resting lightly on Retta's knee. His touch was so warm, so personal, that it stirred a deep longing through her whole body. Yet, she sensed he had become withdrawn, thoughtful, even moody. As she looked at his still profile, she felt alone, puzzled, left-out. She knew he was thinking now of something besides the girl in the red dress who sat next to him in the pickup truck.

When they walked up the flagstone path toward the house, both were aware of movement, the sound of someone pacing about on the side terrace.

Carter Caldwell did not hear them approach. He was alone on an open flagstone porch that had been cleared of redwood furniture for the winter months. His back was to them as he stood next to a low stone wall, a brandy glass in one hand. It was a night of clear moonlight and he seemed to be staring through the big trees, down the corridor of light and shadows, watching the moonlight form a shimmering path on the water of the farm pond. There was something so unexpected, so puzzling about her father, in solitude, looking off into the darkness, that Retta lowered her voice to a whisper when she said, "Poppy?"

Caldwell turned quickly, a half smile on his face, like a man wakened from a dream. "Gad, you two! I didn't expect to see you till all hours. . . ."

"It's almost two o'clock," Retta said. "And Dallas gets to work by six in the morning."

"I just couldn't get to sleep," her father said. He lifted his glass. "I decided on a stiff brandy and some time to myself." He gestured toward the woods and moonlit pond. "I never get tired of looking at that view."

The three of them stood together for a moment,

silenced by their individual thoughts and the beauty of the night. It was her father who spoke first, jarring the moment of magic that had joined them together. Strangely, he spoke almost the same words that Dallas had uttered just a couple of hours ago.

"Well, Dobson," he said. "This prom . . . was it what you hoped it would be?"

Dallas was thoughtful and then said, "This has nothing to do with Retta, remember. She was the prettiest girl there. I wanted her to be happy, but. . . ." He seemed at a loss for words, then he continued, "I don't know what I expected, but I do know it wasn't there. Tomorrow I'll show up at the Kennellys' and I'll do that the next day and the next. And I'll still be a dozen credits short of being a real senior. Nothing's changed. The prom wasn't really *anything*, except to be with Retta. It was just the same people but in fancier clothes. And it was still the school gym, even with some balloons floating around. I thought I would feel *different*. Maybe there's something wrong with me."

Her father's tone was serious, thoughtful. "I think I understand what you mean. For some people, it's never the right time for prom, Dallas. Maybe you're one of them. Maybe you're already too much a man for these things."

"Maybe I'm too old, or maybe I wasn't young long enough," Dallas said. "Whatever my feelings were tonight, they caught me by surprise. At least some of them."

He leaned forward in the moon-touched darkness and kissed Retta — a light, swift kiss on her hair.

"Good-night, and I love you," he whispered. "I love you a lot."

Moments later, she heard the pickup truck pull out the front gate, and the night was so still that she began to wonder if he had spoken at all. Or if those were just words she wanted to hear.

"I'm going to bed now, Poppy," she said. "But I have to ask you something. Why were you waiting up for me, tonight of all nights? Are you worried — about Dallas and me?"

"No, no, it's not that at all," he said. "I don't want you to think that." He took a sip of brandy and then a deep breath. "Retta, your mother wanted to tell both you and Two tomorrow. But I think you should know now. I'm standing here looking out at this magnificent land and a solitude that won't be ours much longer. Mr. Berger called from Philadelphia today. We lost our last appeal to the highway department. They agreed to pay us the minimum worth for our land in a lump sum, but the Zenith bypass is going to come through."

She was torn between searing anger and an acute sense of helplessness. Anger seemed the more stable emotion.

"Why us?" she said bitterly. "Why now? We are all so happy here. Caldwells have always been here. The old cave where Two and I played, the daffodils we planted at the pond, those fir trees that Grand-mama Caldwell put along the drive every year since you were a boy. It's not fair. It can't happen. I can't *stand it* if a highway ruins our lives."

"We *have* to stand it, Henrietta," her father said.

"And I believe we will. Not because we're Caldwells and have strong backbones, but because it's the law. The state has decided that this highway is 'for the good of the people,' and that just proves we're only people, after all. Caldwells can get hurt, too. There's nothing more that your mother and I, or a high-priced lawyer, can do."

Henrietta ran from the terrace and up to her room without turning on a light. Moonlight lay in squares on the floor and she threw herself facedown on the bed, not caring about the new red dress or the fragile flowers on her wrist. She buried her face in the pillow but her eyes were dry, sobs mute. She tried to make her mind as blank as an empty page. She did not want to know or analyze the thoughts that might be there. With so much joy and so much sorrow in one evening, it seemed safer to experience no emotion at all.

Chapter
11

With the beginning of March, several things happened that marred the mood and routine of the Caldwell household. Carter Caldwell flew to California twice in two weeks. The phone number at which he could be reached was scrawled on a pad next to the upstairs phone: Whenever he called home, his wife took the phone into their bedroom, snaking the cord under the door and shutting it tight.

One Saturday morning, a middle-aged man in a business suit came to call and walked through the whole house, room by room, with Mrs. Caldwell. He stayed a long time.

Next Saturday, the same man came again with

two other men and they went through the same careful inspection. "Just business, dear," her mother had said brusquely. "Keep your brother out of our way and I'll explain everything when and if the time comes."

And then there were the strange phone calls, usually late at night. Twice Retta answered, and at her first hello, the calling party hung up.

But it was on St. Patrick's Day, the seventeenth of March, that the first menacing gargantuan highway construction machinery showed up first on the main road and then on the Caldwell property itself. Retta knew she would remember that date forever, not only for the machines, but because Junior Provanza had made everyone laugh at lunchtime by wearing a green felt bowler and matching necktie. And he told Retta similar road equipment had appeared that morning near his father's store.

When she drove home later that day, she saw that the barbed-wire fencing on one side of the meadow had been clipped open. And in another area, a whole stretch of rails from the split-rail fence had been removed and dumped in the roadside ditches.

Day by day, the destruction increased. All the machinery was painted yellow, the bulldozers, trucks, cranes, and power saws. They moved at speed along fence lines, and then turned to bite deeper into the acreage, knocking down trees, clearing away boulders, and scooping up the earth to make an access road. From dawn till near dark, the air sang with the whine of electric saws. Many of the Caldwell trees were so big that they had to be cut down, sawed up, and hauled away before a bulldozer could get through.

To Retta, the huge yellow machines were like things alive, demented dinosaurs that roared and ate the earth closer and closer to the house. Whole stands of trees — birch, oak, wild fruit trees — were snapped off and bulldozed into huge piles, branches interlacing; splayed, twisted roots stretching, turned up to the air. Everywhere was the smell of wet soil and the sick-sweet smell of dripping winter sap.

"Can't we do something?" she asked her mother desperately one day. "Can't we at least cut down our own trees for logs or timber? Must we let everything just be destroyed this way?"

"No, we cannot claim the trees," she said, her face pale and taut. "Your father and I wanted to do that but the answer was no. That land has been condemned. Nothing on it belongs to us anymore."

Retta began to study more and more at school, staying as late as possible, or stopping at the Ambersons', or even driving around the bleak countryside, far from her home, until the yellow machines came to rest for the night. She felt more at peace if she did not have to hear them, even though she knew they were parked out there, somewhere in the dusk. Sometimes Dallas rode around with her until it was time to work at the Kennellys'. They rarely spoke, but he kept his arm around the back of her seat, fingers smoothing her hair or gently touching her cheek, as lightly as a man soothing a kitten.

One late afternoon, Retta took the country lane that passed Little Tennessee, then looped back around the north end of the Caldwell land. The sight was ugly and defeating. Over the past few days, the power saw and big bulldozers had taken down the graceful rim of dogwood and tulip trees that had protected the farm pond and hidden it from sight. It was easily seen from the main road now. It stood raw and naked, its banks bare, the water a turgid snow-gray, with chunks of ice still floating on the surface.

Near them a bulldozer roared along an access road, then disappeared from sight. Dallas said, "Damned cowboys. They don't even know how to drive those things."

And then there was another sound, faint, shrill, and human. It was Dallas Dobson who heard it. "Stop the car," he shouted. "Stop here, Retta!"

She turned off the motor as Dallas leaped from the car, stepped high over a tangle of cut barbed-wire fencing, and raced toward the pond. "We're coming," he shouted.

It was then she saw a little boy, not more than six or seven, standing on the bank, shouting and waving his arms. On the pond nearby floated the old paddleboat, the little pleasure craft she and Two had played with for years. Someone had untied the rope that held it to the pier. Lying on the ground, knocked down by the bulldozer, was a warning sign her brother had made in woodcraft class. Spattered with mud now, the sign still read clearly: NO SWIMMING, NO FISHING, NO BOATING, NO *NOTHING*.

The young boy was close to hysteria. He pointed

111

at the water and sobbed, "My little brother's in there."

The big yellow bulldozer, making a return trip, sighted the figures on the bank. Dallas shouted at the driver, "Get the paramedics! There's trouble here!"

As the driver reached for his two-way radio, Dallas stood motionless for a few seconds, scanning the surface of the gray water, touched into ripples by a breeze and rocking slightly with small, jagged sheets of ice.

Then he pulled off his boots and jacket and dived in quickly, jackknifing through the surface and arrowing toward the muddy bottom. For long moments, Retta could not see him at all. Then he surfaced, sucking in for breath, and dived again.

"Run," Retta said to the young boy. "Tell your daddy to come here."

"My daddy's at work," he said.

"Get your momma, then." She pushed him from behind. "Run! Get somebody!"

The boy ran off toward the direction of Little Tennessee. Dallas surfaced and dived again, so rapidly that she could not see his face or read his eyes. Could he ever find anyone in those murky waters — and in time? Retta was not wearing a watch, but her heartbeats pounded out the seconds and the minutes.

The construction worker came running toward the pond. "I got through," he said. "The paramedics are coming from Zenith."

Water, cold, dark, splashing, closed over Dobson as he dived and surfaced again and again. Then, after an eternity of tension, he surfaced holding a small boy in his arms, a child no more than four years old, limp and inert as a cloth doll.

The highway worker helped to pull Dobson and the unconscious boy onto the bank, saying over and over again, "Help's comin', man. Help's comin'."

Dobson bent over the limp body, clamping his mouth over the little boy's. He sucked in deeply and spat out the pond water that came into his own mouth. Then he laid the child facedown on the bank, head tilted downward, cheek resting on a folded arm, the small, blue-lipped mouth pried open. He knelt over the boy and began a rhythmic pressure on his ribs, trying to press water from the lungs and keep the heart beating. The child's eyes were closed but with each powerful push on his rib cage, a thin trickle of pond water spilled from his lips.

A woman who looked not much older than Retta came running over the muddy field to the pond. She surveyed the scene, her eyes bright with tears, and then said to Retta, "I'm his mama. It's in the Lord's hands. Fall on your knees and pray with me."

The two young women knelt side by side on the damp ground, lips moving with silent pleas. The boy's mother had her eyes shut tight, face tilted toward the sky, and her grip on Retta's hand burned like fire, the sharp, digging nails drawing an ooze of blood.

The construction worker was bending over Dallas, talking in a low, urgent voice, but Dobson never changed his pressure and rhythm. Suddenly, the little boy vomited violently and uttered a single cry of panic.

His mother ran to her son, but Retta stayed on her knees. "We need you, God," she said. "Let him stay alive. Let him be a grown-up boy. All of us want that. God, I'm trying to trust You. . . . Dallas trusts You. . . ."

The thin, urgent wail of a siren snaked through the air and grew louder as it reached the Caldwells' gate. Then the paramedics in their red van made a sharp turn into the meadow, speeded down the lane between the apple trees, and pulled up to the spot where Dallas held the little boy, limp but with his eyes open, holding fast to his mother's hand.

The night darkness seemed to press against the walls of the house, making an opaque mirror of the big front windows, dancing now with the reflection from the fireplace.

Mrs. Caldwell had driven into Zenith with Jimmy-John (the boy had recovered enough to whisper his name to Dallas at the pond) and his mother in the paramedic ambulance. Retta called her father at the newspaper office and explained what had happened. He had driven over to the hospital to meet his wife.

Dallas sat in front of the fireplace, his long arms and legs protruding from one of Carter Caldwell's jogging suits. In the room off the kitchen, the clothes drier still turned, drying out his pond-soaked clothes. His wet boots stood in front of the fireplace, steaming a little in the heat.

"Mrs. Jessup is so grateful to you, Dallas," Retta's mother said.

"We have a lot to be grateful for," Carter Caldwell said. "No way of knowing for sure how long that little tad had been in the water. But the doctors say there is no brain damage. Jimmy-John was sitting up in bed drinking orange juice when we left. All his responses are normal. He'd have been talking his head off if he weren't so shy. The doctor's going to keep him in the hospital a couple of days for observation anyway. He *did* get a lot of cold water in his lungs."

"That poor lady," Mrs. Caldwell said. "Now all she's got to worry about is paying hospital and doctor bills. Her husband is just a part-time picker in a mushroom house."

"But I *told* you," Henrietta said. "The state and the highway department have to take responsibility for *everything*: doctor, hospital bills, and maybe some talks with a good psychologist so that Jimmy-John doesn't go through life with drowning nightmares. Maybe other damages for pain and suffering. That highway worker told Dallas he had asked his boss to replace that fencing and put our warning sign back up. He knew the highway builders had made that pond an 'attractive nuisance,' and that's against the law."

"Do you have the man's name?" Caldwell asked Dobson. The young man nodded. "And what exactly did he say?"

Dallas was silent a moment, then said, "Let me think about it. I'm not quite sure."

"But you told me everything!" Henrietta said. "All you've got to do now is go into town tomorrow and give Squire DeLepino a deposition. Tell him just what you told me. He'll take it from there."

Retta knew she was pressing, that her voice was high and tense, but she had not been able to calm down since the shocking moment when she heard the plea, "My little brother's in there."

"It isn't often that we get a story right on our own property. We'll take a picture of you tomorrow, Dallas, for the front page. Our readers will want to know what a hero looks like."

Dobson seemed uneasy. He passed the back of his hand over his forehead as if he had a fever or felt faint. Mr. Caldwell took over with concerned authority. "We should not underestimate the trauma of what you two young people went through this afternoon. Retta, if you take a hot bath and get into bed, I'm sure your mother will bring you a dinner tray. Dallas, you just wrap yourself in a blanket and we'll get your clothes tomorrow. Right now, I'd like to drive you home."

"But *I* wanted to do that," Retta said.

Dallas shook his head, his face troubled. "Let your father do it, will you?" he said. "And Mrs. Caldwell, could you skip that part in your article with my name in it, especially the hero part? And the picture?"

"We're not on deadline," she answered. "Let's talk about it tomorrow. Are you sure you're well enough to go home?"

He shrugged. "Maybe I swallowed more pond water than I thought. I feel all cold inside."

Chapter 12

N ews of the rescue spread fast through the community. Before breakfast, the phone had begun to ring. Her mother was talking to Mrs. Amberson when Retta waved good-bye and left for school.

She might have been forewarned but she wasn't. She sighted Dallas waiting for her long before she reached the Kennelly gate. He carried no schoolbooks and his shoulders were hunched, both hands jammed deep into his jeans pockets. As she drew up at the side of the road, he signaled her to roll down her window.

"I want to tell you straight off," he said. "I'm not going to Squire DeLepino or anyone else to give a deposition about what happened yesterday. And I'm

not going to have my picture taken for your paper.
It's over and done with. My father doesn't want me
to get involved."

"*Get* involved? You *are* involved. You know something that can help someone else."

"It could go hard for him down at the feed store,
my father says, if word got round that the Dobsons
are troublemakers. He could get fired. We're not
exactly wired in this community, you know."

"But it's the *right* thing to do, Dallas."

"My father doesn't think so and I won't go against
what he says. He's always been square with me."

"I just don't understand."

"All men aren't created equal, my father said that
last night. All men aren't born Caldwells. . . ."

"Will you stop thinking the Caldwells are something special," she said, a new heat in her voice.
"It's Dallas Dobson's turn to stand up and be counted."

He looked at her evenly, his eyes cold and steady.
"Maybe I'm just not ready for that," he said.

They stared at each other for some moments,
stunned at the depth and danger of their anger. Then
he said, "I guess you want me to find another way
to get to school from now on."

"I didn't say that," she protested.

"Not in words," he said bitterly. "Not in words,
but I can read your face, Miss Caldwell. But remember this. He could have given me away when I was
just a kid. But he didn't do that, did he?"

He struck the side of the car suddenly, with the
flat of his hand, a hard, fast blow, like a cowboy
goading a bronco. The sound echoed through the

118

quiet morning woods as sharp as a rifle shot.

Retta gunned the motor and took off alone. Gravel as loud as the sting of hailstones hit the sides and underbelly of the little car as she sped away.

It wasn't that they refused to speak to each other. They just avoided being in the same places at the same time. At lunchtime, Retta was aware he sat at a table in a far corner, bringing his lunch in a brown bag rather than risk meeting her in the cafeteria line. Several times she had sighted him studying in the library, his head resting deep in the cup of his two hands, the palms blanking out his vision on both sides, like a horse with blinders. And Junior Provanza was picking him up at the Kennellys' each morning. Junior's twin sister, Parma, had told her that, putting her arm around Retta's shoulders and whispering, "It's better that you broke up, I think. He's almost nineteen and that's too old for you. And besides. . . ." Retta had moved quickly away and into a classroom.

Evenings were no better. She checked out some Spanish language tapes from the library and played them in her room night after night, eager to hear a human voice, to let it drive away the melancholia that kept splintering her thoughts. The silence of the telephone was maddening, loud as a phantom shriek, echoing through her imagination like a kind of demon. He had never called her at home, she rationalized, and certainly he wouldn't do it now.

Carter Caldwell made a fifth trip to California, and one afternoon, when she called her mother at the newspaper to get permission to spend the night at the Ambersons', she was told Mrs. Caldwell had an appointment at the bank and wouldn't be available until the close of business.

Retta left a note and drove over to Charlie's. She was embarrassed and aware that Mrs. Amberson was treating her differently, soft-voiced and solicitous, offering Retta tea and ginger cookies as if she were some kind of invalid.

Even lying in the twin bed in Charlotte's room, lights out, the radio turned low to a rock station in Coatesville, it was hard to sleep. At midnight, Charlotte said softly, "Don't mind me, Retta. Go ahead. Cry if you want to."

"I don't need to cry," she said sharply. "I have nothing to cry about."

"Sure you do," Charlotte said. "I don't even have a boyfriend and I find something to cry about at least twice a week. A sad song, hurting a sweet nerd like Junior Provanza, my future — we've all got something to cry about."

By midspring the days had stretched longer, so long that the Caldwell family could see the highway damage all around them until the sun faded around seven in the evening. The land stripped of ground cover, the mounds of uprooted and bulldozed trees, the thirty-foot gully behind the house that would soon be a six-lane highway; even the huge yellow road machines were visible from every window, standing silent for the night, like dangerous, lethal insects, caught in a brooding torpor.

"April is the cruelest month. . . ." Those words from the famous poet, T.S. Eliot, ran through Retta's thoughts as she sat at the dinner table one evening. Her father was home again, his face tanned by the California sun, but his eyes were sad; two little lines had etched themselves at the corner of his mouth.

He wants to tell us something, she thought, *something he knows we don't want to hear. This is the way we do things, the Caldwell family. We use the dinner table for our forum, to plan and talk and ask and explain. Careful, civilized, loving each other.* Her heartbreak over Dallas was deep, so pervasive, that she believed she could not be hurt further by anything her father had to say. But she was.

"All right," her father said as her mother passed dessert, plates of fruit and cheese. "It's time we talked. Your mother and I have made some mighty big decisions. We had to. But we still want to hear what you two have to say."

Neither Retta nor her brother moved or spoke.

"This family is going to make a big move. The *Zenith Press* has been losing money, too much money. But we've managed to sell the building and presses to a printing firm. The profits weren't much, but we're lucky to get what we did. And we have arranged to sell this house to a hotel conglomerate."

"Yes," their mother said. "Those men you've seen looking over the house — they've decided to buy it, and what land the highway department left for us, to make into a country motel, the kind of place city folk might like to come for a weekend. They also agreed to buy much of our furniture, a few good

121

antiques, and some other pieces which fit in here and wouldn't be right for where we're going."

"A motel?" Two said in disbelief. "A *Caldwell motel*?"

"Not Caldwell anymore," his father said briskly. "It will be called The Red Fox Inn. The promoters will start with our six bedrooms and three baths, then build a unit for thirty more rooms, extending from the rear of the house. I've seen their plans, and they are going to make a first-class establishment. They expect to enlarge the kitchen, too, and put small tables in this room as a country restaurant."

"My room," Retta said in a low voice. "You mean strangers will sleep upstairs in *my* room?"

Her father nodded. "The buyers liked that room especially, the size, the double views. There is some talk about making it into a country bridal suite."

"But where will *we* be?" Retta asked.

"We will be starting out fresh," her father answered. "The Caldwell family has enough assets to build a small plant and start a new newspaper, plus purchase a good ranch-type house in Thirty-Nine Palms, California. Your mother and I would like to make the move by the middle of May. Before the highway is completed here, and before the summer heat sets in out there. I'll go on out ahead."

"Carter," his wife said gently. "You've forgotten one very important thing." She turned to Retta. "Both you and Two have grown up here on Springhill; but you, Retta, especially, are at an age when old friends are deeply important to you." She paused. "If you *want*, you can stay on here till June, then come back to Havendale High for your senior year. You can graduate with your class and friends. Mrs. Amberson has agreed to have you stay with Charlie and her, just like one of the family. We'd pay room and board, of course, and we'd be generous. Without her job at the *Zenith Press*, the Ambersons will need the money. Would you like that, do you think?"

Retta could think of nothing to say. She was aware of her own silence, then the silence of her parents, waiting for her response. But instead of answering her mother's fateful query, she asked her father a new question.

"Why do they call the town Thirty-Nine Palms? Are there exactly thirty-nine palm trees there?"

He laughed. "Maybe not yet, but there will be. It's a completely new desert development. Kind of an instant city about twenty miles from Palm Springs. Ranch houses, lots of swimming pools, a country club, and three new golf courses. Our newspaper will be the voice of the community from the very beginning. We're taking our talents and skills where the money is, Retta."

Retta knew she had been stalling for time, trying to collect her thoughts and emotions. Her next words were so grave, so portentous that she had to force herself to speak. It was like closing a heavy, brass-bound door, something so strong, so final that she would never be able to open it again.

"You're wrong about my choosing to stay here with friends," she said. "Maybe before, but not now. I want to stay part of this family. . . ."

Later that evening, restless and unable to sleep, Two brought up a couple of soft drinks from the kitchen, then sat at the foot of his sister's bed to whisper in the dark.

"You're coming with us for *sure*?" he said.

She nodded. "But I simply cannot understand what's happening. A full continent away! How can they *do* this to us?"

Her brother was thoughtful, a small, wiry figure hunched up in the darkness. "I think I understand why we must leave, Retta," Two said at last. "It's what Carter needs, mostly. He loves this place so much, and he's loved it *so long* . . . well . . . he can't stand being nearby, can he, Retta?"

Mrs. Caldwell began preparing for the move to the West Coast with her usual efficiency. She bought sheets of colored stick-on dots from a Zenith stationery store and explained her color coding to the family. Blue dots for all the furniture and housewares that were included in the sale of Springhill. Red dots for the give-aways or "maybes," articles that would probably go to a Coatesville auctioneer for resale. And yellow dots for all the "musts," the things the Caldwells loved the most — furniture and family heirlooms — that must make the trip to California.

Local movers came to start packing, and each day, after school, there were fewer books on the shelves, kitchen cupboards were stripped down to a minimum of articles for daily use, and the Gorham silver coffee service was gone from the dining room sideboard.

One afternoon, Retta overheard her mother say quietly to her brother, "Please believe me, Two. I know how hard it is on you and your sister. But those yellow dots you've stuck on *so many* things . . . you've got to thin out your 'musts.' The house in California isn't that big. And we'll be living differently out there."

Chapter
13

After the first of May, decisions and plans became realities. Carter Caldwell closed down the office of the *Zenith Press* and cleared out his big desk in the library at home. He left for Thirty-Nine Palms the next weekend.

In the woods and machine-racked fields around the Caldwell property, activity was stepped up. Now the great yellow machines were visible from the main roads, the side roads, and every window in the house. The great muddy trough directly behind the house was deepening. For Retta, the swift and noisy yellow machines were more than ever like a swarm of demented, uncontrollable hornets, backing and filling in giant clouds of dust, ceasing their erratic destruction only when night fell.

One of the prime chores of the highway workers now was to sort out, amass, and pile up the great jungle of felled timber behind the house. Trees were dragged and pushed and bulldozed over the earth to be heaped into towering piles until there were finally eight massive stacks of trees, thousands in each pile. And around these pyres the bulldozers buzzed and circled, making broad, deep slashes in the earth to act as firebreaks.

"Firebreaks!" Retta asked her mother in disbelief. "They're not going to *burn* those beautiful trees!"

"That's the way they plan to do it. Those trees don't belong to us anymore," her mother said wearily. "But we'll be on our way to the new house before then, Retta."

The following week, two giant moving vans backed up to the Caldwells' front door and began loading the items marked with yellow dots. The air was rancid with the smell of their diesel engines and the big, tripletread tires ripped ribbons of sod out of the front lawn. *T.S. Eliot was wrong,* Retta thought sadly. *April is not the cruelest month. May is worse — much, much worse.*

The moving vans were scheduled to make the cross-country trip in five days, and on the fourth day, Mrs. Caldwell flew out to help set up the new house. Two moved in with friends, since his twin beds had been shipped out, but Retta opted to stay at Springhill alone.

"All right," her mother had agreed with reluctance. "The dogs don't go to the vets for their fly-out trip till next week. They'll keep you company. But I don't want you brooding, Retta. You can keep busy and help me a lot by sorting out the last three trunks of papers and records in the attic. Everything that might be important to the family — birth records, school report cards, anything of that sort — put aside for me. And the rest, including nearly twenty years of those Christmas cards I've saved, just throw them away."

Rainstorms had threatened the area all day, with clouds dark and gray-green as old bruises, and flashes of lightning that ripped open the sky like bright, jagged zippers. At school, Retta tried to concentrate on work, ignoring the heavy overcast that darkened the classrooms, and the damp, raw smell of impending rain. Yet by four o'clock there was a sudden rift in the heavy clouds that showed blue skies. At sunset, the sky was a delicate pink, touched lightly with wisps of white clouds. The storm seemed to have passed.

At nightfall, Retta brought a tuna sandwich and a cup of tea up to the attic with her. She was sorting through the second trunk, half lost in the memories of first grade drawings and children's valentines, when she was aware of someone pounding on the back door, three floors below.

She ran down the stairs and knew, from the sight of his bright yellow hard hat, that the caller at the door was a highway worker.

The man was big and stocky, hair gray under the trim of his hard hat. His voice was careful, almost apologetic, when he said, "I've been authorized to inform you and your family, Miss, that there's been a change in our schedule. You were informed sometime ago that the surplus trees wouldn't be set afire for another ten days. But Official Weather says we've got some wet days ahead. We're going to have enough trouble incinerating green wood. We don't want it wet, too."

"What are you trying to tell me?" she said.

"Well, the total burn-up on those surplus trees can take as long as three or four days. But we want to get started. We've got orders to light up tonight."

Retta closed all the shutters in the house, then made a fresh cup of tea and went back to the attic. Over her head, a single high-watt light bulb swayed on a long cord, sending shifting shadows over the old trunks and the sorted piles of paper.

She no longer knew what time it was, how long she worked alone in the attic when something in the second trunk caught her attention, not because it was conspicuous — but because it wasn't. Her fingers touched several sheets of paper, held together with a rusted paper clip, tucked in the side pocket of the otherwise empty trunk.

As she carefully unfolded the dry, brittle sheets, flecks of paper dropped on her jeans, as light and fragile as flower petals. There was no date, so it wasn't part of a diary. It had no title, so it wasn't a class assignment. There was no salutation or signature so it wasn't a letter. Whatever it was was written in a rambling, loose style, as if someone were talking on paper. The handwriting was not completely familiar. It was somewhat like her mother's but smaller and lighter, with erasures and cross-outs as if the writer did not know quite what to say.

Retta glanced at the first few sentences and then put up her hand to stop the light bulb from swaying. Her tea was cold but she sipped it anyway, glad for the acrid tannic coolness on her dry lips.

Now don't get me wrong, were the first words Retta read. Then:

> *I want you to understand from the beginning that I'm not really dumb. I know what a girl should do and what she shouldn't. I get around. I read. And I have two older sisters. So you see, I know what the score is. It's important that you understand that.*

The next half dozen sentences had been blacked out, so Retta turned the page.

> *You see, it was funny how I met him. It was a winter night like any other winter night. But the way the moon tinseled the twigs and silver-plated the snowdrifts, I just couldn't stay inside. The skating rink isn't far from our house — you can make it in five minutes — so I went skating. But first I borrowed my sister's lipstick and then brushed my hair hard, so hard it clung to my hand and stood up around my head in a hazy halo.*
>
> *My skates were hanging by the back door all nice and shiny, for I'd just gotten them*

for Christmas, and they smelled so queer —
just like fresh smoked ham. My dog walked
with me as far as the corner. She's a red
chow, very polite and well-mannered, and
she kept pretending it was me she liked,
when all the time I knew it was the ham
smell. She panted along beside me, and
her hot breath made a frosty little balloon
balancing on the end of her nose. The night
was breathlessly quiet, and the stars winked
down like a million flirting eyes. It was all
so lovely.

It was all so lovely I ran most of the
way. I had to cut across someone's back
garden to get to the rink, and last summer's grass stuck through the ice, brown
and discouraged. Not many people came
through this way, and the crusted snow
broke through the hollows between corn
stubbles frozen hard in the ground. I was
out of breath when I got to the shanty —
out of breath with running and with the
loveliness of the night.

When I started to skate, it was snowing
a little, quick, eager little soaplike flakes
that melted as soon as they touched my
hand. I waited a moment. You know, to
start to skate at a crowded rink is like
jumping on a moving merry-go-round. The
skaters go skimming around in a colored
blur, like gaudy painted horses, and the

shrill musical jabber re-echoes in the night from a hundred human calliopes. Once in, I went all right.

And then he came. All of a sudden his arm was around my waist so warm and tight, and he said very casually, "Mind if I skate with you?" Then he took my other hand.

That's all there was to it. Just that, and then we were skating. It wasn't as if I had never skated with a boy before. Don't be silly. I told you before I get around. But this boy was different. He was tall, very tall, and at least three years older than I. And he could skate like a professional, almost as if he'd been born to skate with me.

At first I can't remember what we talked about; I can't even remember if we talked at all. We just skated and skated and then we began to laugh at something, and soon we were laughing at nothing at all. It was all so lovely.

Later, we sat on the snowbank at the edge of the rink and just watched. It was cold at first, but pretty soon I felt warm all over. He threw a handful of snow at me, and it fell in a little white shower on my hair. He leaned over to brush it off. I held my breath. The night stood still.

Then he sat up straight and said, "We'd better start home." Not, "Shall I take you home?" or "Do you live far?" but, "We'd better start home." See, that's how I know he wanted to take me home. Not because he had to, but because he wanted to.

It began to snow harder as we walked. Big, quiet flakes that clung to twiggy bushes and snuggled in little drifts against the tree trunks. The night was an etching in black and white. It was all so lovely, I was sorry I lived only a few blocks away. He talked softly as we walked, as if every little word were a secret. He said he thought we should go out again sometime, then something about how nice I looked with snow in my hair, and — finally — had I ever seen the moon so close? A misted moon was following us as we walked, ducking playfully behind a chimney every time I turned to look at it. And then we were home.

The porch light was on and we stood there a moment by the front steps, as the snow turned pinkish in the glow of the colored light and a few feathery flakes settled on his hair. He had been carrying my skates and he put them over my shoulder and said, "Good-night now. I'll call you." . . . "I'll call you," he said.

I went inside then, and in a moment he was gone. I watched him from my window as he went down the street. He was whistling softly, and I waited until the sound faded away so I couldn't tell if it was he

133

or my heart whistling out there in the night.
And then he was gone, completely gone.
I shivered. Everything was quiet.

The last two pages were blurred, almost as if they had gotten damp in the trunk, or someone had cried. From outside, Retta heard a series of distinct but muffled sounds, like the bursting of distant balloons or the cottoned puff of explosions.

She laid the last handwritten pages on the floor, and used her finger to trace them word for word, forcing meaning from the smudged pages.

And that was two months ago, the writing said, *two months ago last Thursday. Tonight is Tuesday, and my homework's done, and I darned some socks that didn't really need it, and I worked a crossword puzzle, and I listened to the radio, and now I'm just sitting. I'm just sitting because I can't think of anything else to do. I can't think of anything — anything but snowflakes and ice skates and yellow moons and that Thursday night. The telephone is sitting on the corner table with its old black face turned to the wall, so I can't see its leer. I don't even jump when it rings anymore. My heart still prays, but my mind just laughs. Outside the night is so still — so still I think I'll go crazy — and the white snow's all dirtied and smoked into grayness, and the wind is blowing the arc light so it throws weird, waving shadows from*

the trees onto the lawn — like thin starved
arms begging for I don't know what.

There was a sudden increase of light in the attic, as if a surge of energy had gone through the light bulb. Retta looked up but the bulb was just as it had been before, no brighter, no less.

The last lines of the page were written in a hasty scrawl, as if the effort to put the words down had become too sad for the writer to bear. They read:

And so I'm just sitting here, and I'm not
feeling anything. I'm not even sad, be-
cause all of a sudden I know. All of a
sudden I know. I can sit here forever, and
laugh and laugh while the tears run salty
in the corners of my mouth. For all of a
sudden I know. I know what the stars knew
all the time; he'll never, never call — never.

Retta sat motionless, wondering what it was she had read, and who was speaking out with such heartbreak, almost like herself, from those old pages.

Then she became aware of intense heat and a light film of sweat on her forehead. Something had happened, something had changed. A spasm of panic clutched her throat. She folded the pages together, put them in her jeans pocket, and ran to an attic window. A loose shutter moved under her fingers and she pushed it outward into the night.

Behind the bulldozed firebreaks and stretching over hundreds of yards were eight huge bonfires, so alive with licking, biting flames that they seemed to have a life of their own, like demons, malevolent and tortured.

From the intensity of the blazes, Retta judged that the wood had been doused with flammable liquid before lighting. That would account for the small, muffled explosions she had heard as each mound was lit and burst into flames. Already slender limbs had begun to buckle with heat and fall back into the fire. Bunches of flaming leaves burst off the branches and sailed into the night sky. It was as if everything she had known all her life was going up in an inferno.

As she ran downstairs and toward the fires, she knew she was crying because her eyes stung with tears, but it was anger, not sorrow, that was her deepest emotion.

She hurried down one of the plowed-up auxiliary roads until she was in a direct line with the conflagrations, facing one of the blazing heaps of brush and timber. Then she stopped short, feeling the heat scorch her cheeks and turn tears dry and sandy on her eyeballs. The trees seemed like living things to her, writhing and collapsing in the flames, and the fire was noisy, both crackling and sucking, as it consumed the timber. The acrid smoke smelled of whatever kind of tree was burning — wild apple, cherry, spruce, or king maple — and the air was sweet and pungent with the smell of scalding sap.

She was so consumed with anguish and horror at what was happening that she did not hear a car nor the footsteps of Dallas Dobson until he seized her by both shoulders and forced her to move back from the flames. She fought him with fury, pounding at his chest, kicking against his hard cowboy boots, crying in soft, breathy sobs like an exhausted child. She knew she was hysterical, almost out of control, but it seemed that nothing could stop her pain.

He held her tight, trying to pinion her arms with one of his own, using his free hand to smooth her hair and touch her cheek with his fingertips. "Charlie called me. Provanza called her. The fires are lit on their land, too." And then his voice was low, no more than a whisper, a little singsong of love and comfort. "I couldn't let you be alone, baby," he said again and again. "I couldn't be away from you."

He turned with her in his arms so his body was between her and the flames. Her emotions were so taut, so raw, that she did not completely register the change from anger and hysteria to the new passion that gripped her. She moved closer to him, touching his face, feeling that she could never kiss him enough. As she reached up, he put his big hands at her waist to support her, and she seemed to sway on the tips of her toes, barely touching the earth.

Without speaking, in a mutual motion as fluid as if they were one body, they sank to the ground, never losing their embrace, never breaking their kiss. Retta believed with all her soul that she was ready for what now seemed inevitable.

It was Dallas Dobson who broke the spell. He sat up suddenly and put his head in his hands, like a man in despair. For moments he was silent, and then, as she sat up beside him, he took her hand and kissed the palm, as if he were laying some golden promise within her grasp. But his voice was taut with bewilderment and emotional pain.

"Retta," he said, "trust me. This is all wrong for us. It *can't* be this way. I *can't* be a spoiler like my father. . . ."

If they spoke after that, she couldn't remember, but she felt her thoughts, her breathing, become more calm, more rational. They sat apart, not touching, but neither made a move to go back to the house. They turned to look at each other at the same time and she tried to smile. In the blaze of the firelight, she saw him as through a screen of red, every feature distinct but enlivened with brilliance. In his eyes she could see a tiny, quivering reflection of the flames and knew he must see the same fires as he looked at her.

Chapter
14

The two days that followed had the fragmented, painful quality of a nightmare. Powerful things were happening to Retta and her life. She knew this was true but could not trust herself to believe it. The dogs, badly frightened by the fires, stayed close to the house, whimpering and panting. Retta set out a pan of water for them before leaving for school each morning.

Other farms with condemned lands had had their trees set to burn. For miles around, the air was flecked with bits of charred ash and the thin trail of smoke curved all the way from the outskirts of Zenith and off into the distance where the proposed highways snaked toward Baltimore.

At school on the last day, Retta checked her locker for forgotten library books, got a month's refund on her parking slot, and turned in her current texts. During that final lunch hour, Mr. Engel led her classmates in a farewell cheer that ended, "Retta! Retta! Rah! Rah! Retta!"

Dallas Dobson sought her out between classes, just to walk a few steps together, and sat at her table at lunchtime, looking at her, watching her face.

"No way? You're sure there's no way you could stay?" he asked the last day.

She shook her head. "Mother got back from California yesterday. Our plane tickets are for tomorrow." Then she answered his question before he spoke it. "Leaving is hard enough, Dallas. I don't want you at the airport. Please."

Yet it was more than her own immediate feelings that bothered Retta. The strange bit of writing, so akin to her own fears, burned in her mind. She put the pages in an envelope and set them on the fireplace mantel in the front hall.

There was no longer food in the refrigerator, and since Two was going to the airport with friends, Retta and her mother had dinner in the front hall, perched on packing barrels, with hero sandwiches Mrs. Caldwell had bought at Provanza's.

In the early evening, the phone rang constantly from family friends wanting to say a last good-bye. Charlie Amberson called three times, the last to ask if Retta would fly back from California to be maid of honor if Charlie got married, or even had a date for that matter. Maryanna Nairn, a nearby neighbor, stopped by with a dozen daffodil bulbs dug up from her own garden. "When they bloom in California, remember us," she said, then ran to her station wagon in tears.

It was nearly midnight before Retta could find the quiet moment she needed to question her mother. At last she turned from a packing barrel and said, "We can't do anything more tonight, except this, Mother."

Retta went to the mantelpiece and picked up the envelope with the tattered pages.

"I want you to tell me what it means." She slipped the pages out of the envelope and handed them to her mother.

Connie Caldwell drew in her breath sharply and took the fragile pages carefully, as if they might be hot to the touch. She sank down on the edge of a packing crate. "From where, Henrietta?" she said. "I haven't seen these pages for years."

"In a trunk in the attic. I found them just before . . . just before the fires were lit."

Connie Caldwell and Retta studied each other for a moment, and then Mrs. Caldwell said, "I hope you will try to be understanding. These pages are about something that happened to me a long time ago."

"But it's not a diary, it's not a story. What is it?"

"It was a report to a doctor."

"Were you ill?"

"Yes, but in a very special way. What happened in those pages happened to me. I tried to put it down just as I remembered it, just as I felt it."

Mrs. Caldwell put a hand over her eyes, then shook her head, as if she had found a thought there she couldn't tolerate. She looked squarely at her daughter. "Remember, I was Connie Jagerfeld then, just a small-town sixteen-year-old, living with her family in Zenith. It just happened. I went skating one night, met a boy who almost changed my life. I can't say I simply fell in love. It was more than that. I was infatuated, I was obsessed. I could think of nothing else. My own feelings got beyond me.

"As those pages tell you, I waited more than two months for a phone call. It was too much for me. In those days, one couldn't easily discuss problems with parents. Or my older sisters, for that matter. Anyway, I just didn't have the words. I couldn't sleep. I couldn't eat. And suddenly I began to cry, alone, in school, in crowds, for no reason I could put my finger on. I was melancholy, deeply, deeply depressed."

"Are you sure you want to tell me this?" Retta asked.

"Perhaps I should have told you before," her mother said. "But at sixteen, I didn't know where to turn, so I made an appointment with our family doctor, old Doctor Felix. I went secretly, after school. I tried to explain to him that I was sick because I was in love. Good, kind, dear man — he thought I meant I was pregnant."

"And were you?" Retta said.

Her mother smiled a little and shrugged. "One evening together. . . . Except when the boy and I were skating together, we didn't even hold hands. . . . When I told Dr. Felix that, he said to me, 'Maybe it would help if you wrote it all down. Tell me in your own words what happened, how you feel. Then maybe I can help you.' "

"And that's what's on those pages?"

"Yes," her mother said. "I cried so hard that sometimes I couldn't see the paper, but I got it all down."

"And?"

"I brought my thoughts to Dr. Felix the next week. I sat in his big chair, watching him as he read, but I couldn't tell from his face what he thought.

"When he finished, he returned the pages to me and said, 'This will be between you and me, Connie. Your broken heart, I don't have any medicine to cure that. Maybe you can help yourself. My diagnosis is that you're a damned good writer. Make that talent work for you.' "

Her mother laughed lightly. "You know most of the rest. I forced myself to apply for a job on the school newspaper. I wrote girls' sports news for two years, then I was promoted to editorial. The editor of the paper finally asked me for a date. And that's how I got to know Carter Caldwell."

"And the other person, the boy you wrote about. Did he ever call you?"

"Back then, do you mean?"

"Back then."

"Yes, he did. About four months after that night at the skating rink. Gossip moves fast in a small town. I almost guessed what he wanted. The girl he'd been dating — they'd had a falling-out that night at the skating rink — was pregnant and wanted him to go away with her, leave town. He said that if I'd date him, if I'd pretend I was his girl all along, he could claim he wasn't the father. I told him I would never do that."

"And?"

"He and the girl left town. It was over as far as I was concerned. I heard they had gone somewhere down South."

For Retta, the small pieces of coincidence and fate were locking themselves together, piece by piece, into an almost complete picture. It was more than just Dallas and she. She remembered now the concern, the questions her father had asked her the morning after they had found the little fox together. And her mother's behavior that first night when Dallas stayed for dinner. The bright eyes, the pearls, the music, the candlelight.

"And that person from long ago," Retta said, trying to conceal the tremor in her voice. "You know where he is *now*, don't you, Mother? And he *did* call you again. . . ."

"Yes, to both questions. He called me some months ago and said he wanted to see me. He asked me to meet him in Zenith." Mrs. Caldwell began to pace the brick-floored foyer, short, quick steps that telegraphed her inner agitations. "I told him I would never do that."

"And he kept calling?"

"I'm not sure, but I think so. Remember those late-night calls we've been getting? Someone either says 'wrong number' or just hangs up? I think that's who's calling. That would be his way."

"And, Mother, that night of the big snowstorm, when Dallas had dinner and stayed the night with us. . . . Am I right about this? Your party clothes, the special dinner, the way you acted . . . that wasn't just for Dallas, was it?"

"He was a guest in our house. I wanted him to see us at our best. I wanted your friend to like me. . . ."

"But it wasn't *all* for him alone, was it? You wanted him to tell *someone else.*"

"That could be true, Retta. Some hurts are very deep. I suppose — in my secret heart — I may have wanted him to tell someone else about that evening."

Retta paused to be sure her voice was under control. Then she said, "The boy you loved so much — that was Danny Dobson, wasn't it?"

Mrs. Caldwell nodded. "It was Danny Dobson."

"And you didn't think I should be told about it?"

"Retta, please. Remember I said I hoped you'd be understanding. . . ." Her mother took a deep breath, then continued. "I didn't know that Danny Dobson had another son after Sam Houston. For weeks I didn't even know you *knew* someone named Dobson. I didn't hear of it until your father told me, after the night the two of you found the fox.

"But I'd noticed changes, your daydreaming, your new quietness, the look in your eyes after you'd been studying over at Charlie's. Then I learned there was a new Dobson in our lives. I realized what you must be feeling. I believed I owed you silence, a chance to make up your own mind. And I needed time myself to think about Connie Caldwell, to be sure my own scars were healed."

Retta got to her feet and put out her hand to stop her parent's pacing. For the first time, she realized she was taller than her mother.

"Please," she said softly. "I *do* want to understand. But I need the absolute truth. Why are we doing all this? Mother, have we changed our lives because a highway came through our farm — or are we moving to California because Danny Dobson is back?"

Her mother's words were suddenly strong and sure. "Listen to me, Henrietta, and believe me. I am going to California because the man I love is there. In everyone's past, there is *some* pain. Mine was deep. Maybe I hung onto it too long. But I know myself. I married the man I love, deeply and truly. I haven't lived a lie these past twenty years."

The only phone still connected was in the upper hall, and when it rang, Retta Caldwell said, "That must be for you, Mother. No one would call me this late at night."

Mrs. Caldwell frowned, looked puzzled, then waited till the phone had rung three times before going up the stairs. Retta heard a few muffled words, then her mother's voice. "It's for you, Henrietta. Danny Dobson's son wants to talk to you."

As Retta picked up the phone, she heard a bedroom door down the hall close softly and realized with a heartbeat of gratitude that her mother was granting her privacy.

Dallas's voice was deep and resonant. "I'm calling

from the phone booth outside Provanza's market," he said. "The damndest thing has happened." A pause. "Are you there, Retta?"

"Yes, yes. What is it you want to tell me?"

"I was thinking about you so much, I just couldn't stay home. So I've been driving around for hours in the pickup. Finally I went home and turned in the drive without lights because I didn't want to wake my father. Then I went into the front room and I hadn't switched a lamp on yet. I was just standing there, thinking. Then I heard a noise upstairs that I couldn't figure out."

"What was it?"

"I had to find out, so I went out the back door and climbed onto the porch roof. I never made a sound, Retta. I crawled over to my father's bedroom window and looked in. I guess he thought I wasn't home yet. I nearly fell off the roof. He had a drink in his hand and his crutches were over on the bed. He was talking to himself and *walking back and forth.* Not even a limp. That man can walk, Retta! Can you hear me, my father can *walk.*"

"He can *walk?* Without crutches? The pain, the limping, they weren't *real?* All this time he's just been *pretending?*"

"The important thing, Retta, is that man can *walk.*"

"But he's lied to you. Over and over again, he's lied to you, Dallas. Don't you see that? He bullied you, made you pity him. He didn't give you a real chance, did he? And you're not *angry?*"

"Right now I'm too stunned to be angry. I'm confused. He must have been afraid to level with me.

After Sam Houston, he must have been afraid I'd leave him, too. I don't think it matters too much why he lied to *me*, Retta. But how could a man do that to *himself*?"

Retta realized her breathing had become fast and shallow, touched with panic. She ran the tip of her tongue lightly over her dry lips before trying to speak. "What does this all mean, Dallas?"

"To us or to him?"

She paused. "To him, I guess."

"I'm not sure, Retta. I've got to think. But I didn't want you leaving for California without knowing what I know. . . ."

At ten o'clock the next morning, the plane left from Philadelphia airport enroute to Los Angeles, with a connecting flight to Palm Springs. Mrs. Caldwell had asked for three window seats so each of them could say his own farewell to the sprawling mass of Philadelphia and the green fields and thick woods of Pennsylvania.

As the plane climbed for altitude, Retta looked down, her forehead pressed against the small oval of the plane's window. Directly beneath her she could see the big-city mixture of glass-cube architecture and placid older streets lined with the red brick of Colonial architecture. The plane was still low enough to cast a ground shadow over the parks and the broad, blue ribbon of the Delaware River.

The big airship arced west, passing in moments over the farmlands and winding country roads immediately outside Zenith. Retta peered down intently, trying to find landmarks, but at the plane's altitude, cars disappeared, woods became brushlands, and roads and fences faded from view. The route of the new highway was clear. She saw the raw, stripped earth and the bonfires that sent up sharp beacons of light, like mirror reflections, and a smudge of fire-cloud that followed the long, curved route of the bypass like a thin, gray boa of smoke.

Retta closed her eyes. There was no use hoping, no use straining. She could distinguish nothing below, fence or field, that had, for nearly seventeen years, marked off the place she'd called home.

Chapter
15

There were eight other recently finished houses on the street called Desert Lily. The Caldwells' was the last one, on a corner lot, a sprawling new adobe house with a low front wall and sliding glass doors on all three bedrooms, leading out to a pink cement patio that matched the decking around the pool.

Everything was new, from the jacuzzi whirlpool in the master bathroom to the trash compactor in the kitchen that bagged and crushed household garbage with jaws of steel. Except for three transplanted palm trees, tall and graceful, the back garden was not landscaped, but Mrs. Caldwell had made a bright, clay-pot garden at one end of the pool with summer zinnias and white-flowered periwinkle that bloomed and flourished in the desert heat.

At night the family gathered for dinner around a glass-topped table on the patio. Mrs. Caldwell tried such recipes as snow crab with lobster sauce, avocado stuffed with chicken, shrimp with Japanese vegetables, and a bean curd called "tofu."

The sun seemed to glare down from the sky from six in the morning until nearly eight at night, when the stars came out, brilliant in the clear desert atmosphere.

Unlike the countryside, neighbors here were close. From their garden, the Caldwells could not only see the lights of neighboring houses but they could often hear the murmur of voices. After one "California dinner" of barbecued beef with alfalfa sprouts and pita bread, Two said in a loud whisper, "Mother, isn't there such a thing as a *potato* in this state?"

Thirty-Nine Palms was ringed on three sides by high, stark mountains, monoliths of granite as dry and formidable as the desert floor. They made a dramatic background to the brilliant green of golf courses, the blue sparkle of one pool per house, and the graceful groupings of palm trees. There were masses of planted flowers everywhere, attracting green and purple hummingbirds, darting and sucking nectar, looking like flying blossoms themselves.

For the first two weeks, Retta wore sunglasses, even inside the house, and kept her bedroom draperies drawn. "Could it be possible that California could be too beautiful?" she asked her mother. "Couldn't it rain just a *little*?"

Her yellow car had arrived and sat baking in the desert sun. A Pennsylvania student transferring to Stanford had driven it west. The sight of it brought Retta close to tears.

Her brother was embarrassed at having made two "bicycle friends" the first day, two young teenagers who lived a block away. They took him first to the just-opened, air-conditioned mall with thirty shops, plus fountains, and gardens under glass. And they also showed him how to hike the faint desert trails that led to small oases, and even how to find the hidden waterfalls not far from Palm Springs.

One afternoon, Retta herself made a solo trip to the mall, but felt like an alien under the lofty skylights, with the moving ribbons of escalators and the huge, indoor potted trees. Everyone her age seemed to be wearing cut-off jeans with tank tops and sandals, bodies sunburned to an even caramel, with sun-bleached hair and eyes blocked out by huge sunglasses. No one had the kind of face she longed for: strong, weather-beaten, and with green-brown eyes that wanted to see and be seen.

There had been no phone call from Dallas Dobson.

One night on the terrace, Two whispered to her, "Why don't you call *him*, Retta? We all know how much you're hurting."

"I can't," she said simply. "It wouldn't be the same."

As each blue-sky day and starlit night passed, Retta felt more remote from the joy and security of the familiar Pennsylvania life. Whatever it was, she hadn't been able to hold it. It had eluded her.

One night in bed, she turned her thoughts into prayers and said ruefully, "Listen to me, God. This is a multiple-choice question. Are You going to break my heart till I can't stand it anymore? Are You going to help me to forget him? Or are You going to let him find me again?"

Somehow she had not thought of a letter. Her brother signed for it and brought it to the luncheon table on the terrace. "For you, Retta," he said. "Air Express. That means it cost him almost ten dollars and he had to drive into Zenith to mail it."

It also means, she thought as she took the envelope, *that less then twenty-four hours ago, Dallas Dobson stood in the post office in Zenith. And this letter was in his hands.*

In the solitude of her room, Retta pulled the draperies just a little, enough to send a shaft of light across the letter. It was short, just two pages, written in strong, black letters, as if the writer were hunched at a table, pressing the urgency of his words onto the page.

Dear Henrietta:

I did three things since I saw you. And I want you to know. First, I went to Squire DeLepino and gave him a deposition on what happened down at the pond that day. I gave him the name of the hard-hat and the license number on the bulldozer. Squire says the man won't be hard to locate. And with my sworn statement, and whatever else he can get, the Jessups have a good case.

Second, I talked with my father. I told him I knew he could walk if he wanted to, and I told him how I found out. He was angry at first, then scared. I know he wanted to shout or punch me across the room — or go out and buy a bottle, but he didn't. He let me talk and then he talked. We talked like people, like friends. I told him that wherever I was, I'd still be with him because I love him. I told him how much it meant to me that he kept me, that he never put me out to be someone else's son.

Today is the first day he went to work without crutches. He promised me he's going to try to get his act together and I believe him, Retta. He has to, in fact, because I made it clear I was leaving him for three months, crutches or not.

And the third thing, and I need your help on this, Retta. I got a copy of Arabian Horse Times *from Mrs. Curtayne. I knew she'd subscribe. There was an ad in the classifieds. A ranch between Palm Springs and Indio is looking for summer help. I called the number and talked to a Mr. Bradley at Rancho Arabian. He *and his wife own the place. I told them what I know about horse care and how much I wanted the job. But they didn't want to hire me over the phone. So I told them about you. Can you drive out to Rancho Arabian and pin down the work for me? I hope you will do that. The ranch is listed in the phone book.*

I'll have to be back here to finish up and graduate in the fall, but if I get the job, we can have almost three months together. I could leave here next Tuesday, and when we circle over the desert, I dream I'll see that little yellow car coming to meet me. I have the money for air fare, you know. My father won't need that operation.

If I'm saying too little, Retta, it's because there is so much to say. We need this time together, don't we? And it's right that I come where you are.

If the Rancho Arabian folk don't want to hire me, I'll have to face that. And if you won't want me to come, I'll have to face that, too. But I'll never believe it. You have my phone number.

> *(I'll say it when I see you —)*
> *Your friend,*
> *Dallas Dobson*

They could see her at four o'clock, the Bradleys said on the phone, and told her how to proceed to Bob Hope Drive, make a right turn off to Ramon, and then make a left turn when she got to Desert Moon Road. Drive all the way out, first on blacktop, then dirt. Make a right where the dirt road ends and go through the double gates. That's where the Rancho Arabian acreage begins, and the only house and barns one can see are ours.

Both Bradleys were waiting for her in the cool, rambling ranch house. She was aware of big leather couches, bright paintings, cowhide rugs, and the soft hum of air-conditioning. The Bradleys were a young couple, in their midthirties, and almost look-alikes with blond, cropped hair, jeans, and range boots. Both were so tanned that their eyes looked blue-painted in their faces.

Retta followed and listened as they showed her first the apartment for the new horse man — a small, neat two rooms and bath, just off the main house. Then they walked over sandy gravel paths to the outdoor pens, split-railed squares with corner bubblers of fresh running water in each and a shady overhead protection of sheeted, corrugated iron for the horses. A huge tom turkey with dusty feathers and scarlet wattles followed them everywhere, squawking and scolding.

"We call him Doctor Vet," Mrs. Bradley said with a laugh. "He looks out for the Arabians almost as carefully as we do."

"We would want your boyfriend to remember that horses need special attention in sun country," Mr.

Bradley said. "These Arabians are highly sensitive to sunburn. They can get in just as much trouble as human beings."

"Oh, I'm sure he knows something of that from Texas," Retta said quickly. "He's been around horses since he was a little boy." She was impressed with the Bradleys' attractive and efficient operation. She wanted them to feel she truly represented Dallas Dobson. She wanted them to trust her. Therefore she tried to make the tour of the ranch without her sunglasses, so she could look at the Bradleys in a direct and straightforward manner, but the temperature was in the high nineties and the bright glint of sunlight off the sand and shale were too much for her.

On the fence of each outdoor stall was a placard stating exactly how many pounds of hay and pellet supplements were to be given to each horse. "We want someone as dependable as a time clock. These horses are on a rigid schedule. We haul their feed to them twice a day, exactly at six A.M. and six P.M. We don't want any colic or barn fever. Do you think your friend is trustworthy?"

Retta told them about the snowstorm, the Kennellys' old Arabians, and the back-country skiing. "In all the time I've known him," she said, "he never missed a day at work. Sometimes he even worked two jobs."

Inside the long, cool barn were a dozen top-breed Arabians, ranging in color from a dun brown to a light gray, almost silver in the dim light of the stalls. As the Bradleys' footsteps sounded out on the concrete floor, each horse in turn put its head over the half door, whinnying and stomping, waiting to be caressed and talked to. Only one mare got the voice treatment without hands-on attention. Because she was allergic to the bite of a certain desert gnat, the horse was stalled behind tight, heavy screening and only taken out to air in the cool of the evening. Another Arabian wore a headdress of beaded strings to flick away flies that caused infections to its sensitive eyes and ears. The headdress swung and rattled every time the horse moved its head. Two of the younger horses had playthings in their stalls, big wooden apples, painted red, hanging from the roof by a rope.

"The young ones can get so bored cooped up in this hot weather without something to play with," Mrs. Bradley said. "We expect your boyfriend is genuinely fond of horses. These highly bred animals need a lot of attention. They seem to know they're valuable."

Retta told them a little about Dallas's background with rodeos in Texas, how much he had learned from his father. "I think he not only loves horses, he respects them. He thinks they are splendid animals."

"What's most important to us," Mr. Bradley said, "is someone not only with knowledge and barn skills, but one who has that extra something, a person who can look at a horse, touch it, and say with confidence, 'That animal is in good health.' My wife and I travel a lot in our business, and we want someone with enough savvy and common sense to recognize trouble when he sees it, and call the vet."

Retta tried, as courteously and frankly as possible, to answer all the questions they asked, and to fill in what she thought they should know about Dallas Dobson.

At the end of the tour of barn and equipment buildings, they walked to the big outdoor exercise ring. It was empty now, baking in the late afternoon sun. "Whomever we hire is going to spend a lot of time in this ring," Mr. Bradley said sternly. "And we'll expect him to adapt to our desert hours. Now, he *will* have use of our pickup truck. He won't be bound and tied to this place. But we expect long hours and we want a horseman who can adapt."

"Please tell me what you mean," Retta said.

"In this summer heat, we can't exercise the horses in the daytime. It's too much for them. Your friend Dobson will have to work out a schedule for our approval. The horses can be exercised *only* before six in the morning and *after* nine o'clock at night. You'll notice this ring has special incandescent blue lighting. That's so the horses won't see shadows to stumble over, even their own. I'd expect Dobson to keep on the job, no matter how late, till each horse has its daily workout."

Mrs. Bradley looked at Retta, a question in her eyes, and when Retta said nothing, the woman said, "But I don't see why you couldn't help him. Or just be with him while he works the horses. Maybe he's like an Arabian himself. Maybe he likes company."

Retta looked around at the ring with its white

wooden fences, screened-in viewing porch, the big lights, and the coiled lunge-lines for exercising. "You have an elegant operation here," she said. "Anyone would be proud to fit in."

"And one last thing we'd better discuss," Mr. Bradley said. "It's of prime importance. We have a four-teen-year-old son, Burton. He's in school right now, but he's beginning to be an expert horseman and we want him to continue that way. And we want him to learn everything possible about Arabians and the operation of this ranch. We'd expect Dobson to answer questions, give orders when necessary, and make use of the talents of a lively fourteen-year-old. Do you think he has the patience for that?"

"I'm sure of it," Retta said with enthusiasm. "He would like it very much, I think. He had a brother himself, you see, an older brother who — " She stopped, surprised at the catch in her voice. "What I mean to say is, he liked his older brother so much, I'm sure he'd remember how Sam Houston treated him."

Mrs. Bradley put her arm around Retta's shoulder, then turned to her husband. "That settles it, darling, don't you think? Dallas Dobson is the right man for the job."

Mr. Bradley put out his big hand to Retta and said, "Let's shake on it, Miss Caldwell. Tell your boyfriend we'll expect him next week."

"And if we like him half as much as you do, my dear," Mrs. Bradley said, "we've got a gem."

* * *

Retta put a glass of ice water beside the phone and watched the clock. She had decided to dial the number at the exact moment of six.

After her interview with the Bradleys, she had come home to tell her mother that Dallas had the job. Then she showered, changed into fresh jeans and shirt, and touched cologne to her hair. It was almost as if she were going to see him in person, and she could not quiet the rapid beat of her heart or the turmoil in her thoughts. Dallas had the job. He had the right to know that as soon as possible. The sound of his voice and how she reacted to that voice would be her lodestar, the key to the important words she wanted to say next.

In far-off Pennsylvania, the Dobson phone rang four times, and then a fifth before a man answered it.

"My son's not here, Miss Caldwell," Danny Dobson said evenly. "He's still over at Squire De-Lepino's. Left here about an hour ago. The Jessup case. But you know all about that."

"Yes, I do," she said.

"Well, they rounded up that highway worker to make his own statement," Dobson said. "And to validate what Dallas already had to say."

"Then can you do this for me, please, Mr. Dobson?" she asked, "Take down this number to be sure he has it. Tell him to call me tonight. I'll wait up till I hear from him."

"Can't you give me the message?"

"No, I'd rather talk to him directly." She gave Danny Dobson the California phone number and waited for a response. Then, into the silence, she said, "Are you sure you have the number correctly? Are you sure you'll give him my message tonight?"

Danny Dobson's tone was sardonic, even amused, but she sensed the hurt in his voice. "Don't worry, Miss Caldwell. Even a broken-down cowboy's got some sense of honor."

Carter Caldwell had stayed in Thirty-Nine Palms to have dinner with his new advertising manager, and his family ate a nearly silent meal on the patio. They were all caught up with the tension of waiting, the acute sense of seconds ticking by.

Night in this part of the desert came abruptly, when the sun slipped behind the looming mountains and snuffed out the day. Tonight it left brilliant streaks of red and pink, edged with a spreading gray at the horizon.

By eight o'clock the table had been cleared and the Caldwell house was quiet. Retta sat with her mother and brother in the dusk, looking out over the desert garden. New fruit trees had been planted and the miniature limes gave off their sharp, juice-green odor in the cool of the evening. There was a half moon, pale as a night moth, and its thin light gilded the three palm trees and imprinted their slender shadows like an etching on the surface of the swimming pool.

It was after eight o'clock, which meant it was after eleven in Pennsylvania, and still Dallas Dobson had not called.

"He *will* call, Retta, I know it," her mother said quietly. "This is different."

From off in the distant night, somewhere at the foot of the mountains, came a high, eerie yapping, the sound of a wild coyote pack on the prowl. The loneliness, the feral abandon in their call, made Retta shiver. She folded her arms around herself in a kind of hug, hoping to draw confidence from the warmth of her own body.

"My friends tell me there used to be hundreds of coyotes round here," her brother said. "With all the building, they've had to find new feeding grounds nearer the mountains." He peered at his mother and sister through the darkness. "My friends say that water is the big problem. Sometimes they come down in the night, dozens of them, and drink out of swimming pools."

Retta said nothing, absorbed in her own thoughts. Her brother turned to her and said, "Coyotes mate for life. Did you know that, Retta?"

"Oh, Two," she said helplessly. "I know you're trying to be helpful, but you're just making things worse.

"And you, Mother," she said, "you're no help *at all*. Just saying over and over again that he is going to call doesn't make it *happen*. What do you really and truly think about his coming here? I know what *I* think — but can't you tell me your thoughts? Can't you be of some help? What am I starting here? I don't even know how this thing is going to *end*. . . ."

"No one ever does, Retta," her mother said. "Love — even a chance at a little happiness — it's always a gamble. It's all up to you and Dallas. No one else, absolutely no one else can — " Her mother stopped, listening.

Then they all heard it. Inside the house a phone had begun to ring.

MAUREEN DALY was a high school student when she launched a brilliant writing career with "Fifteen," a story for which she won third prize in the Scholastic Writing Awards Competition. She was still a teenager when she published her first short story, "Sixteen." When she wrote *Seventeenth Summer,* her landmark young adult novel that went on to be a bestseller, Maureen Daly was not yet twenty.

About *Acts of Love,* Ms. Daly says: "I was inspired by the deepest joys of my daughter, Megan. And by that summer in the small Pennsylvania town when she defied the building of a highway and fell in love with a young man who cared deeply about the things she cared about."

A novelist, journalist, and screenwriter, Maureen Daly has traveled extensively. She has written several works of nonfiction for adults and is the author of a collection of short stories for teenagers. Ms. Daly lives and writes in Palm Desert, California.

point®

Other books you will enjoy,
about real kids like you!

☐ 42365-7	**Blind Date** R.L. Stine		$2.50
☐ 41248-5	**Double Trouble** Barthe DeClements and Christopher Greimes		$2.75
☐ 41432-1	**Just a Summer Romance** Ann M. Martin		$2.50
☐ 40935-2	**Last Dance** Caroline B. Cooney		$2.50
☐ 41549-2	**The Lifeguard** Richie Tankersley Cusick		$2.50
☐ 33829-3	**Life Without Friends** Ellen Emerson White		$2.75
☐ 40548-9	**A Royal Pain** Ellen Conford		$2.50
☐ 41823-8	**Simon Pure** Julian F. Thompson		$2.75
☐ 40927-1	**Slumber Party** Christopher Pike		$2.50
☐ 41186-1	**Son of Interflux** Gordon Korman		$2.50
☐ 41513-7	**The Tricksters** Margaret Mahy		$2.95
☐ 41546-8	**Yearbook II: Best All-Around Couple** Melissa Davis		$2.50

PREFIX CODE
0-590-

Available wherever you buy books...
or use the coupon below.